The Investig of Edgar Drake

Secrets of the Old Lancaster Mansion

Genevieva

Copyright © Genevieva, 2025. All rights reserved.

No part of this book may be reproduced, stored in a retrieval system,

or transmitted in any form or by any means without the prior written permission of the author.

This is a work of fiction. Any resemblance to actual events, locales, or persons, living or dead, is purely coincidental.

Published by Genevieva

2025

Table of contents

Introduction 3
    Chapter 1: Mystery Behind Closed Doors 7
    Chapter 2: Secrets Under the Veil of Mist 61
    Chapter 3: Morning Reveals Its Secrets 73
    Chapter 4: An Evening of Secrets 91
    Chapter 5: Hidden Past 103
    Chapter 6: Illegitimate Legacy 112
    Chapter 7: The Will and Its Consequences 124
    Chapter 8: Edges of Truth 136
    Chapter 9: Unmasking 159
    Chapter 10: Invisible Clues 178
    Chapter 11: Concealed Traces 193
    Chapter 12: New Revelations 215
    Chapter 13: The Final Exposure 244

Introduction

The old Lancaster mansion stood on a remote hill, surrounded by dense woods, giving it a majestic yet somewhat gloomy atmosphere. The house had been built over a hundred years ago, and its grand architecture, with tall windows and massive columns, had long symbolized the Lancaster family's prosperity. But today, the shadows hanging over the house were darker than usual—Richard Lancaster's funeral had brought all the family members back under one roof.

The day was gray and rainy, as if the sky itself mourned the departed. Cars arrived, and members of the Lancaster family, dressed in black coats and hats, quietly climbed the stone steps of the mansion to pay their final respects. Inside, a dim light illuminated the rooms, and tension filled the air, becoming more palpable by the hour.

In the spacious parlor, where the farewell ceremony took place, an oppressive silence reigned. The coffin containing Richard Lancaster's body stood in the center of the room, surrounded by flowers. Relatives and close friends whispered quietly to one another, while some simply sat in silence, their heads bowed.

Lady Evelyn Lancaster, Richard's widow, sat on the edge of a chair, staring tensely at a single point. She clutched a small black handkerchief, constantly squeezing and unfolding it. Her face, usually cold and unreadable, seemed even more severe today.

Beside her, arms crossed, stood her son—Andrew Lancaster. He was tall, fit, with a serious expression on his face. His eyes reflected deep fatigue, mixed with irritation. He glanced slowly at his mother, then at his cousin, Simon Lancaster, who stood by the window, holding a glass of whiskey.

"Do you think he left us anything?" Andrew whispered quietly, leaning toward his mother.

Evelyn pressed her lips together and said nothing. She knew the question was rhetorical.

Simon, a young man in his 30s with dark hair and piercing blue eyes, nervously rubbed his temple. He was known for his temper and greed, making him unpopular within the family. He clearly wasn't mourning his uncle's death; rather, he seemed anxious, as if something important was looming in the air, something he eagerly anticipated.

At that moment, the parlor door quietly opened, and Geraldine Lancaster, Simon's ex-wife, entered. She appeared focused and wary. Her dark hair was neatly styled, and her eyes restlessly scanned the room. She froze for a moment, looking at the coffin, then confidently walked over to Simon.

"I'm surprised you came, Simon," she said quietly, but there was a faint sharpness in her voice. "I thought you were too busy with your affairs."

Simon gave her a disdainful look, slightly raising one eyebrow.

"Geraldine, I always make time for important events. And this event, whether you like it or not, concerns me more than it does you, doesn't it?"

She squinted slightly but held back her response. Edgar Drake, a quiet observer standing nearby, noticed the sudden tension between them, and in his mind, this became the first clue.

The next day, everything was supposed to return to normal. The morning was even gloomier than the day before, and no one seemed to be in a hurry to leave the Lancaster house. Around 10 a.m., a piercing scream broke the silence of the house.

It was Lucy Lancaster, Richard's youngest daughter. She ran down the hallway, trying to find someone who could help. Horror was etched on her face.

"Simon... He's dead!" her voice broke into sobs.

Everyone quickly gathered in the upstairs study, where Simon's body was found lying on the floor. His face was twisted in a final expression of pain. The police soon arrived, and the formal investigation began.

Without hesitation, the police called in Edgar Drake, who by then was well known for his brilliant investigations. Edgar arrived at the mansion within an hour, his stern face reflecting calm, and his eyes immediately began scanning the surroundings.

He slowly examined the body, taking his time before making any conclusions. Then he stood up and addressed those present:

"I understand this is a shock for everyone. But as you know, I'm not here for comfort. I'm here to find out what happened. And I won't leave until the truth is uncovered."

Chapter 1: Mystery Behind Closed Doors

The clouds over the Lancaster mansion grew heavier, shrouding the house in an oppressive gray mist, as though shielding it from the outside world. Inside, a suffocating silence reigned, broken only by the muffled voices of police officers. A faint scent of aged wooden panels mingled with the damp earth brought in from outside.

Edgar Drake, a tall man with short dark hair and piercing gray eyes, stood by the study window, staring at Simon Lancaster's lifeless body sprawled on the floor. His expression was calm, as always, and his movements deliberate and measured. Dressed in a dark jacket and tailored trousers, Edgar exuded professionalism and composure. His brows knitted slightly as he studied the scene, sensing a discrepancy in the narrative forming before him.

News of a death at the Lancaster mansion spread like wildfire. The relatives, who just the day before had been mourning at a funeral, now found themselves embroiled in yet another tragedy.

"Well, Mr. Drake, what do you think?" The voice of Officer James Miller, a short, stocky man with graying temples, snapped Edgar out of his thoughts. Miller stood by the door, visibly uneasy.

Without taking his eyes off the body, Edgar replied curtly, "I think we're dealing with murder. And it was well-planned."

Miller tensed. Deep down, he had suspected as much but had clung to the hope of a more mundane explanation—perhaps a heart attack or an accident. Edgar's words dashed that hope entirely.

"Murder?" Miller lowered his voice. "Are you certain?"

"For now, it's a hypothesis," Edgar finally turned to face him. "But I rarely err in such matters. Especially when there are several suspects from the outset."

Miller frowned. Suspects? He hadn't even interviewed everyone yet. How could Edgar already form suspicions? But the detective's expertise and reputation left little room for doubt. Miller took a deep breath, deciding against probing further.

"All right. I'll see to it that everyone in the family remains in the house until the investigation is complete."

"That would be wise," Edgar said simply, resuming his examination of the room.

He stepped toward the desk at the center of the study. At first glance, everything appeared orderly—no papers or items suggesting a struggle or haste. But his attention was drawn to a small stack of letters in the corner of the desk. Edgar leaned down and carefully picked one up.

"Personal correspondence?" Miller asked, stepping closer.

"Possibly," Edgar opened the envelope and skimmed the contents. It was a routine business letter, yet something about it struck him as peculiar. He set it aside, resolving to revisit it later.

"Who was the first to find the body?" Edgar asked sharply, without looking up.

"Lucy Lancaster, Richard's youngest daughter," Miller replied. "She discovered it around ten this morning. Claims she had just entered the study to speak with her cousin when she found him dead."

"She's hiding something," Edgar muttered. "It's time we had a word with her."

Lucy Lancaster, a tall, slender young woman with wavy blond hair and striking blue eyes, sat in the grand drawing room. Clad in black, her pale face betrayed her inner turmoil. Her hands nervously fiddled with the hem of her dress, and her gaze darted around the room, avoiding direct eye contact.

Edgar entered quietly, his footsteps muffled by the plush carpet. Lucy's eyes flicked up to meet his as he approached.

"Miss Lancaster, I need to ask you a few questions about what happened this morning."

Lucy nodded, though it was clear she was struggling to maintain her composure.

"I... I only wanted to speak with him," she whispered, barely holding back tears. "I don't even know how this could have happened..."

Edgar sat across from her, maintaining enough distance to avoid overwhelming her, though his eyes were fixed on her face.

"Please, tell me exactly what happened," he urged gently.

Lucy took a deep breath, gathering her thoughts.

"I went to the study around ten this morning, as usual. I... I knew Simon was there alone and wanted to discuss the inheritance with him. We've all been on edge since Father passed away. When I entered, he was lying on the floor. I... I knew immediately he was dead."

Her voice broke, and she buried her face in her hands.

"When was the last time you spoke to him before this morning?" Edgar asked, giving her time to compose herself.

Lucy looked up, confusion flickering across her face.

"Yesterday. We barely exchanged words during the funeral. Simon was always... in his own world. But I never thought he could..." her voice trailed off.

Edgar observed her reaction closely. She seemed shaken, but there was something unnatural in her demeanor.

"Did anyone else know you planned to speak with him today?"

Lucy shook her head.

"No, it was spontaneous. I just wanted to clear up a few matters."

Edgar nodded but mentally noted the suspicious smoothness of her account. Rising to his feet, he said, "Thank you, Miss Lancaster. That's all for now. Please don't leave the premises; we'll need to speak with you again."

Lucy nodded again, remaining silent.

As Edgar left the room, he encountered Miller in the hallway.

"What do you make of her?" the inspector asked, watching Edgar intently.

"She's hiding something," Edgar replied tersely. "But I can't say what just yet. We need to speak with the others."

Leaving Lucy Lancaster behind, Edgar stepped into the mansion's long, dim corridor. The muffled footsteps of the police only deepened the ominous silence of the house. This old, gloomy home held many secrets, and now it fell upon Edgar to uncover which of its inhabitants was complicit in Simon Lancaster's murder.

Stopping by a window, Edgar's gaze swept over the misty garden stretching beyond the house. The sky, shrouded in gray clouds, drizzled rain against the glass. His thoughts lingered on his recent conversation. Lucy was hiding something, that much was clear. But what? And why?

Suddenly, the familiar creak of a door echoed down the corridor. Edgar turned to see Inspector James Miller approaching, his usually composed face etched with uncertainty and his thick brows furrowed in frustration.

"I've just finished questioning Geraldine Lancaster," Miller said as he drew near. "She claims she hasn't seen Simon since this morning. But... she had motives, didn't she?"

Edgar nodded.

"Yes, her divorce from Simon wasn't amicable. Financial disputes, rumors of infidelity... But that alone isn't enough to prove her guilt."

Miller frowned deeply.

"Then who?" his voice cracked with exasperation. "It seems everyone in this house could have had a reason to wish him dead."

Edgar turned to the inspector, his piercing gaze seeming to unravel the truth behind the words.

— This is a house full of secrets, Inspector. If someone here killed Simon, they planned it meticulously. It's crucial not to overlook a single detail.

Miller pressed his lips together, noticing how Drake's calm demeanor contrasted with his own inner tension. Suddenly, Edgar turned on his heel and headed toward the door to the drawing room.

"I need to speak with Geraldine as well," he said.

The drawing room was cool, with dim light filtering through thick curtains. Geraldine Lancaster sat on an antique sofa, her hands nervously clutching a teacup. She was a slender, graceful woman in her early thirties, with smooth chestnut hair neatly styled into an elegant bun. Her refined features—high cheekbones and a delicate nose—showed signs of fatigue and strain. Her dark eyes seemed deep, as though concealing some sadness. An elegant black dress accentuated her figure and understated style, but her slender fingers fidgeting with the cup betrayed her anxiety.

At the sight of Edgar, she stiffened slightly.

"Mrs. Lancaster," he began, stepping closer. "I have a few questions for you."

Geraldine set the cup down on the table, glancing nervously at the detective.

"Of course," she said, attempting to appear composed, though her hands betrayed her nerves.

"You told Inspector Miller that you hadn't seen Simon since this morning," Edgar continued. "Can you clarify what time you got up?"

Geraldine paused to think.

"I didn't sleep well. I woke up early, around six. I went to the garden to get some air."

"And were you alone there?"

"Yes. There was no one else in the garden," she replied, though Edgar detected a note of uncertainty in her voice.

"The garden is quite large," he observed. "You couldn't have seen everyone."

Geraldine bit her lip, realizing he'd caught the inconsistency in her statement. She looked back at Edgar.

"What are you implying, Mr. Drake? Are you suggesting I might be hiding something?"

Edgar leaned forward, his voice soft but probing.

"I'm not drawing conclusions prematurely. But you know the relationship between you and Simon was strained—divorce, financial matters, shared connections... Who do you think might have wanted him dead?"

Geraldine sighed, lowering her gaze.

"Everyone in this house... Each of them had a motive, even if they don't want to admit it."

Edgar paused for a moment, then rose.

"Thank you, Mrs. Lancaster. I'll speak with you again later."

He exited the room and returned to the corridor, meeting Miller along the way.

"What's next?" the inspector asked, still tense.

Edgar stopped and looked at Miller.

"We need to question everyone. But the key is finding the links between them. They all had motives, but not all of them are directly tied to Simon. Whoever killed him knew something that none of us does—yet. And I intend to find out what that is."

Edgar slowed his pace, contemplating his next steps. This house, full of hidden connections and secret motives, was becoming increasingly complex to navigate. He understood that time was on his side, but not indefinitely. He needed to piece together the chain of events before one of the suspects panicked and tried to cover their tracks.

Suddenly, a figure appeared at the far end of the corridor. It was Evelyn Lancaster, the widow of Richard Lancaster—a woman of strict principles and iron will. Even now, after all the tragedies, she maintained an air of composure and cold calm. Her black hair was neatly styled in a classic updo, emphasizing her status and elegance. Her sharp features—deep-set eyes and sharply defined cheekbones—made her look like a sculpture. She walked slowly, as if weighed down by grief, but held her head high, as though she were still the mistress of the house.

Edgar stopped and waited as Evelyn approached. She halted in front of him, her face betraying no emotion.

"Mr. Drake," her voice was low and calm, but tinged with weariness. "I hear you've started questioning people. What happens now?"

Edgar sensed a hint of tension in her voice, though she tried to conceal it.

"Yes, Mrs. Lancaster. We're speaking with everyone to understand who might have been involved in what happened. We need to find out what happened to your nephew," he replied calmly, careful not to pressure her but remaining direct.

Evelyn froze for a moment, her eyes narrowing slightly.

"Nephew..." she repeated softly. "I wouldn't say Simon and I were close. He was more connected with Richard and Andrew. But still..." She trailed off, seemingly searching for the right words.

Edgar didn't interrupt, giving her time to collect her thoughts.

"This house has seen much grief, Mr. Drake," she continued. "First, my husband's death. Now this. I'm no longer sure who in our family can be trusted."

Her words made Edgar wary.

"Do you think someone in your family might have been involved in Simon's death?"

Evelyn froze, then lowered her gaze.

"I don't know..." she said quietly. "Everyone in this house has secrets."

Her words were laden with hidden meaning. Edgar realized it was more than just a passing remark. With every conversation, the picture grew more tangled, but at the same time, clearer. Edgar nodded and leaned slightly closer.

"I'll need to speak with your son, Andrew. Where can I find him?"

Evelyn raised her eyes.

"He's likely in the library. Andrew often retreats there when he needs to be alone."

Edgar thanked her and headed toward the library. The Lancaster mansion was a labyrinth of hallways, each leading to its own secluded corner. He walked slowly, mentally reviewing the information he had gathered. With every step, he felt the atmosphere of the house grow more oppressive. At that moment, he realized time was working against them— the longer the investigation dragged on, the more desperate the killer would become to conceal the truth.

When he reached the library door, he paused, gathered his thoughts, and quietly opened it.

Andrew Lancaster, a tall man with close-cropped hair and sharply defined features, sat in a deep chair by the fireplace. His eyes were fixed on the flames, and he held a glass of something strong in his hand. Like his mother, Andrew always appeared composed, but now his face showed exhaustion and a hint of suppressed anger.

Edgar stepped into the room, and Andrew slowly turned to him, his gaze cold and empty.

"Mr. Lancaster," Edgar began. "I have a few questions for you."

Andrew raised the glass to his lips and took a small sip, his eyes never leaving the detective.

"Questions?" his voice was low and quiet. "You want to talk about Simon?"

Edgar nodded and moved closer.

— Yes. We need to understand what happened to him. Who might he have been in conflict with? And what could have driven someone to murder?

Andrew leaned back in his chair, his eyes clouded over.

— Simon was... a difficult man. At first, he was like a brother to me, but over the past few years, something changed. He became different. Greedy, envious. There was something dark in him.

Edgar nodded, listening intently.

— Did you have any conflicts with him recently?

Andrew thought for a moment, then shook his head.

— No. We didn't argue openly. But he knew I was unhappy with how he handled the family assets. He wanted too much for himself. And I think that was his undoing.

Edgar studied Andrew carefully. His voice lacked emotion—he spoke as if recounting a settled fact, as though he had long since said goodbye to Simon in his mind. Something about it struck Drake as unnatural, but he refrained from drawing conclusions.

— Wanted too much for himself, — Edgar repeated. — What exactly do you mean?

Andrew, after taking another sip, shrugged slightly.

— Money, of course. Lately, Simon had been engrossed in financial schemes. He was trying to push me out of the family business. I'm sure if it weren't for that, he would have continued his usual dealings. But he crossed a line.

— In what way? — Edgar asked calmly.

Andrew paused for a moment, then shook his head.

— Honestly, I don't fully know what he was planning. But I had a sense it involved our father's inheritance. He was always envious and greedy. And that greed ultimately led to his downfall. But I can't say I'm surprised. He made many enemies.

Edgar nodded silently. Andrew seemed distant about his cousin, showing no warmth but also no overt hostility. Still, his indifference felt strange—after all, Simon was family, despite their troubled relationship.

— So, Simon had enemies, — Edgar concluded, gazing thoughtfully at the fire in the hearth. — But who do you think could have gone so far?

Andrew smirked.

— You're probably expecting me to say it could have been me, aren't you? — his voice was laced with sarcasm, but his eyes remained cold. — But no, Mr. Drake, I didn't kill Simon. I had enough reasons to dislike him, but not to that extent.

— Then who do you think could have done it?

Andrew frowned and leaned forward slightly, placing his glass on the table.

— Anyone, — he said quietly. — In this house, everyone has something to hide, their own little secret. Even you, Mr. Drake, I'm sure, have skeletons in your closet.

Edgar didn't react to the jab. Instead, he analyzed Andrew's every word and expression, trying to pick up on any clues to the truth.

— Perhaps, — he replied calmly. — But this isn't about me right now. You say everyone has something to hide. Even your mother?

Andrew tensed.

— My mother has nothing to do with this, — he replied, more sharply than Edgar had expected. — She's been through too much lately. I don't think she could be involved in something like this.

Edgar observed Andrew silently, noting the change in his tone. His defensive reaction to a question about his mother was unexpected.

— Very well, Mr. Lancaster. Thank you for your time. I won't keep you any longer. — Edgar stood, and Andrew returned to staring vacantly at the fire.

When Drake left the library, he met Miller waiting for him in the corridor.

— Well? How's it going? — the inspector asked, his face tense with anticipation.

— He knows something but is hiding it, — Edgar replied, calmly observing the hallway. — But he's not directly involved. At least, it seems that way. His anger at Simon is real, but not murderous.

Miller nodded, though his expression showed he wasn't satisfied with the answer. He was clearly ready to suspect everyone.

— So, who's next? — he asked.

Edgar Drake thought for a moment.

— We haven't spoken to Martin Hudson yet, — he reminded. — He was a close friend of the family and managed Richard Lancaster's finances. He knew Simon, and financial matters often play a key role in cases like this.

Miller nodded, agreeing with the conclusion.

— Then he's our next candidate, — the inspector said, turning toward the staircase.

Edgar followed, his thoughts already moving to the next phase. Martin Hudson, an experienced lawyer, had managed the Lancaster family's finances for years. It would be interesting to uncover what lay beneath his professional façade.

Martin Hudson was waiting for them in his office, located in a wing of the estate far from the main family quarters. The room was tastefully decorated: wood-paneled walls, a massive mahogany desk, and several shelves lined with legal books and old documents. Hudson was a man of order, and it was reflected in his surroundings.

When Martin Hudson rose to greet them, Edgar noted his poised demeanor. Martin was a middle-aged man with a sharp gaze and neatly trimmed hair. His carefully groomed appearance and tailored dark suit reinforced his image as a serious professional. Hudson always gave the impression of someone in control, but now there was a flicker of unease in his eyes.

— Mr. Drake, Inspector, — he began with a slight nod, — how can I assist you?

Edgar sat across from him, while Miller remained standing nearby.

— We need to ask you a few questions about your acquaintance with Simon Lancaster, — Edgar said, watching closely for any reaction.

Martin nodded, placing his hands on the desk.

— Of course. I've known Simon for many years. We worked together, you could say. I was his lawyer and handled his affairs, as well as those of his father, Richard.

— When did you last see Simon? — Miller asked, crossing his arms.

Martin thought for a moment.

— We met a few days ago. We were discussing the inheritance. Since Richard's death, Simon had taken a greater interest in family matters. He wanted control over some assets he believed were rightfully his.

Edgar made a mental note, listening.

— And how were your professional relations with him? — Edgar inquired.

Hudson leaned forward, his expression serious.

— Honestly, they were complicated. Simon was ambitious and impatient. He wanted everything immediately. Sometimes, I had to rein in his desires, which, of course, didn't always please him.

— Rein in? — Miller repeated.

— Yes. For instance, he wanted expedited access to certain financial resources without waiting for the proper legal procedures to conclude. That could have caused legal issues. He was frustrated, but as his lawyer, I had to act within the law.

Drake glanced at Miller, who also caught the key detail—Simon might have been under financial pressure.

"Do you know if anyone else was interested in these assets? Someone who might have had a reason to want Simon... gone?" Edgar asked cautiously.

Martin's gaze briefly grew more intense as he looked at the detective.

"In this house... everyone. Every single one of them had their reasons to care about the family's money. Simon annoyed more than just Andrew. Evelyn was also concerned about his ambitions, though she tried not to show it. And Geraldine... she was always at odds with Simon, especially after their divorce."

Edgar noted how Hudson began mentioning other family members but kept his thoughts to himself.

"And yet," Edgar pressed, leaning slightly forward, "who do you think had the most significant conflict with Simon?"

Martin hesitated, his eyes lingering on the table for a moment before meeting Edgar's again.

"I'm not sure. But honestly, I think Simon's own actions and greed brought about his downfall. He made too many enemies."

Edgar nodded and rose to his feet.

"Thank you for your time, Mr. Hudson. We'll get in touch if we have any further questions."

Martin Hudson nodded slightly in response, remaining seated as Drake and Miller left the study.

In the corridor, Miller frowned.

"Something's off here. Hudson is clearly holding something back," he muttered.

Drake glanced at his partner, then back at the door to the study.

"Perhaps. But one thing is clear—Simon didn't leave anyone indifferent in this family. They all had reasons to suspect each other, and everything revolves around these financial schemes."

Miller nodded in agreement.

"So, what's next?" he asked.

Drake paused for a moment, considering his next steps.

"We need more time to piece the full picture together. Everyone has motives, but no one has solid evidence pointing to guilt. It's time to dig deeper."

The two walked silently toward the staircase when Lucy Lancaster appeared on the second floor. She looked even paler than when they had first spoken to her. Her eyes seemed to dart around, as if searching for something in her mind. When she saw them, her lips trembled slightly.

"Mr. Drake..." her voice was quiet but filled with anxiety. "Have you... found anything yet?"

Edgar stopped and looked at her.

"We're continuing the investigation, Miss Lancaster. How are you feeling?"

Lucy nervously swallowed, her hands clenched into fists.

"I feel like everything is falling apart. There's something wrong in this house..." She glanced around, as if afraid someone might overhear. "I... I feel like someone is watching me."

Miller frowned slightly, while Edgar remained composed.

"Who do you think might be doing that?" he asked gently.

Lucy flinched and lowered her gaze.

"I don't know... I'm not sure. I just feel it. Since Simon's death... everything's different. Maybe it's just my nerves, but I can't shake this feeling."

Edgar considered her words for a moment, then stepped a bit closer.

"Lucy, you mentioned wanting to discuss inheritance matters with Simon. What exactly were you concerned about? Could it have influenced his actions?"

Lucy froze for a moment before her gaze dropped again.

"I knew Simon wanted more than he was entitled to. We all knew. But I didn't think it could lead to..." She trailed off, leaving the sentence unfinished.

"To what?" Edgar asked softly.

Lucy lifted her head and met his eyes.

"To murder. I didn't think anyone would go that far."

Edgar sighed, sensing the tension rising in her voice.

"Someone wanted to stop Simon. Maybe because of his ambitions, or perhaps because he knew something that could harm the others," Edgar said thoughtfully. "Did you have disagreements with him?"

Lucy nodded, trembling slightly.

"Yes. We weren't close. But... I would never have done this," her voice cracked, and she lowered her gaze again. "You can ask Geraldine. She knew more than the rest of us."

Hearing Geraldine's name resurface only deepened Edgar's suspicions.

"Very well, Miss Lancaster. Thank you for your honesty," he said softly. "If you remember anything else, please don't hesitate to reach out."

Lucy nodded, though her eyes remained dull, as if she was trapped in a constant state of fear. She turned and walked away slowly, leaving Edgar and Miller alone.

Miller turned to Drake.

"What do you think?" he asked, narrowing his eyes slightly.

"Her fear isn't fake. But something in her words makes me think she's still holding something back," Edgar replied quietly.

Miller sighed, letting his arms drop to his sides.

"Another person who seems to be hiding something. This is starting to feel like an endless chain of lies."

Edgar nodded.

"Lies are part of human nature, Inspector. But the trick is figuring out which of these lies leads us to the truth."

Miller gave a silent nod before looking back at Edgar.

"So, who's next? Anyone we haven't spoken to yet?"

Edgar paused for a moment, thinking.

"Geraldine. We need to question her more thoroughly. She keeps coming up in conversations. Simon was her ex-husband, and their relationship wasn't exactly smooth. She might have motives she hasn't revealed yet."

Miller nodded, and the two headed toward the room where they believed Geraldine might be.

When they reached the door, Edgar knocked cautiously.

"Come in," a soft voice called from inside.

They entered to find Geraldine Lancaster seated in an armchair, staring out the window. She turned slowly as they walked in, her face calm, but her eyes betraying a hint of unease.

"Mrs. Lancaster," Edgar began, taking a seat nearby, "we have a few more questions."

Geraldine nodded, though her gaze remained distant.

"Of course. What do you want to know?"

Edgar paused, studying her calm face, which seemed like a mask concealing inner tension. He understood that Geraldine had mastered the art of composure, but her eyes betrayed her unease.

"Mrs. Lancaster," he began, "Simon was your ex-husband. Could you tell me about your relationship with him after the divorce?"

Geraldine turned away from the window and looked at Edgar. A shadow of sadness flickered across her face, but she quickly regained control of her emotions.

"Our relationship was... complicated," she said slowly. "After the divorce, I tried to keep my distance from him. It was hard for both of us. But I wanted to maintain neutrality for the sake of the family and to avoid creating more problems."

"What made the relationship so complicated?" Edgar pressed.

Geraldine hesitated for a moment. "Simon was a man who didn't know limits. In the beginning, he was charming, but over the years, everything changed. He became cold, obsessed with money and power. He always felt shortchanged, as though he wasn't appreciated enough in the family, and that created a lot of tension."

Edgar nodded, listening intently.

"Am I correct in assuming financial matters also played a role in your divorce?"

Geraldine gave a brief nod. "Yes. He was consumed by money and business. I tried to support him, but eventually, he started seeing me as an obstacle. He believed I was preventing him from achieving what he thought he deserved."

"And after the divorce? Did you stay in contact?" Edgar continued.

Geraldine frowned, as if trying to recall details. "Rarely. Only when it concerned family or property. I tried to keep my distance, but it wasn't easy, given that we all remained connected. Sometimes I saw how his ambitions pushed him to the brink."

"Did you know about his plans regarding the inheritance?" Miller asked, breaking his silence for the first time.

Geraldine glanced at the inspector, her expression becoming more guarded. "Of course, I knew. Simon always believed he deserved the lion's share of the inheritance after Richard's death. It was an obsession of his. He wanted to control everything that belonged to the Lancasters."

Edgar noticed the bitterness in her tone.

"And how did you feel about those ambitions?"

Geraldine sighed, her gaze drifting back to the window. "I thought it was madness. I tried to convince him that money and power couldn't replace family relationships. But he wouldn't listen. He was blinded by his desire for control. I knew it would lead to trouble eventually."

Edgar listened closely, sensing genuine regret in her words, yet there was something more beneath the surface.

"Mrs. Lancaster," he said gently, "are you aware if anyone threatened Simon in recent days? Or perhaps he mentioned feeling unsafe?"

Geraldine turned sharply, her expression darkening.

"Threatened?" she repeated, surprised. "No, he never told me anything like that. But..." she hesitated, as though unsure whether to continue.

"But what?" Edgar leaned forward slightly.

Geraldine furrowed her brow, looking down at the floor. "Lately, Simon had become even more paranoid. He talked about someone in the family betraying him. He didn't name names, but I could tell he was on edge. It was strange... even for him."

Drake and Miller exchanged glances. Her words hinted at something significant.

"Thank you, Mrs. Lancaster," Edgar said, his tone sincere. "This is important information. We may need to follow up with additional questions."

Geraldine nodded silently, her face calm, but something flickered in her eyes that Edgar couldn't quite decipher.

As they left the room, Miller turned to Drake. "She definitely knows more than she's letting on. But for the life of me, I can't tell what," he muttered.

Edgar nodded in agreement. "She knows more, but something's holding her back—fear or guilt, perhaps. We'll press further, but for now, we should speak to someone else."

Miller raised an eyebrow. "Who's next?"

Edgar stopped at a window, staring thoughtfully at the misty sky. "Evelyn Lancaster. She's been hiding something from the start, and her reaction to questions about Simon's family relationships was far too composed. I need to hear her version of events."

The two men headed toward the wing where Evelyn's quarters were located. The mansion was enormous, and each step echoed through its empty corridors. The silence of the house, broken only by their footsteps, hinted at how many secrets it still held.

When they reached Evelyn's door, Edgar knocked softly. There was no answer. He knocked again, louder this time, but still no response. Miller glanced at the detective with concern.

"Something's not right," Miller said quietly.

Edgar frowned and, after a brief pause, cautiously pushed the door open. It creaked as it swung inward. The room was dim, the heavy curtains blocking out the sunlight. Edgar stepped inside and scanned the space.

Evelyn sat in a large chair by the window, motionless, like a statue. Her face was pale, her eyes fixed on some distant point, her hands resting quietly on the chair's arms. She didn't react to their presence.

"Mrs. Lancaster?" Edgar called softly.

Evelyn slowly turned her head, her gaze seeming far away.

"What do you want, Mr. Drake?" she asked, her voice quiet but cold.

Edgar moved closer, taking a seat across from her, while Miller remained by the door.

"We need to ask you a few questions, Mrs. Lancaster. It's about your nephew's death."

Evelyn closed her eyes for a moment, then exhaled slowly.

"Simon..." she said, a trace of sadness in her voice. "I always knew he would face trouble sooner or later. He was too ambitious. Too greedy. But I never thought it would lead to his death."

Edgar studied her carefully. Her voice sounded weary, but it was too restrained for someone mourning a loved one.

"Tell me about your relationship with Simon," he requested.

Evelyn didn't answer immediately. Her gaze remained fixed on the window, though she seemed not to see what lay beyond.

"Our relationship was always strained," she finally said. "He was the son of my husband's brother, but he never saw me as a legitimate member of the family. He always viewed me as an obstacle, someone standing in the way of his plans. But I tried to remain neutral for the sake of the family."

"Did he accuse you of anything?" Edgar asked cautiously.

Evelyn was silent for a moment before nodding slowly. "He didn't trust me. In recent months, Simon became suspicious of everyone. He was convinced someone was trying to take away what he considered his. Maybe he was right. But I never openly opposed him."

"And yet he saw you as a threat?" Edgar pressed, leaning slightly closer.

Evelyn met his gaze, her eyes hardening. "I always opposed his methods. But I wasn't a threat to him. He created his own enemies. Money, power—it all consumed him. He built his own downfall. And if someone killed him, it was one of those he betrayed."

Edgar exchanged a look with Miller. Her words sounded like justification, as if she was preemptively absolving herself of blame.

"Who exactly might he have betrayed?" Miller asked, stepping forward.

Evelyn sighed. "This house holds many secrets, Inspector. And many people who want more than they have. Simon was just one piece in this game."

"And what can you tell us about the others?" Edgar asked. "Andrew? Geraldine? Who, in your opinion, might have been involved?"

Evelyn tightened her grip on the armrests, her face remaining impassive.

"Andrew... he always envied Simon a little. But he's not capable of murder, I'm sure. As for Geraldine... their marriage was a disaster from the start. But she's too clever to take such an open risk."

Edgar stood, realizing it wasn't the right time to ask more questions.

— Thank you for your answers, Mrs. Lancaster. We may come back to you later.

Evelyn didn't say anything, merely turning back toward the window, lost in her thoughts. Drake and Miller left the room, leaving her in silence.

As they closed the door behind them, Miller let out a quiet sigh.

— Every conversation makes things more tangled. It seems everyone had a motive, yet no one admits anything.

Edgar pondered for a moment.

— They're all hiding something. But Evelyn is right about one thing — Simon made enemies for himself. We need to continue questioning...

Drake and Miller walked slowly down the mansion's long corridor. Miller broke the silence.

— So, what's next? Do you think it's Geraldine? Or Andrew?

Edgar walked alongside him silently, his face focused.

— Everyone in this house has secrets, — he finally said. — But I'm not sure we're any closer to solving this. I feel like we're missing something crucial. All the suspects act like they're protecting something, but it might not be related to Simon's murder. We need to dig deeper.

Miller smirked.

— Aren't we already digging deep enough? They're all hiding something, and each of them has a motive. You've seen their looks. No one's telling the truth.

Edgar stopped and looked at Miller.

— That's true. But the more I listen, the more I'm convinced the real motive might not be what it seems at first glance.

Miller frowned.

— So what is it? Jealousy? Betrayal? In this house, anything's possible.

Edgar thought for a moment before answering.

— I don't know yet. But something is bothering me. Someone here is manipulating everyone else. And I'm determined to find out who it is.

Suddenly, footsteps echoed from the far end of the corridor. Approaching them was Amelia Harper, the late Richard Lancaster's personal assistant. Amelia was an attractive woman in her mid-thirties with slightly curly blonde hair that fell in soft waves over her shoulders. Her usually calm gray eyes now seemed wary and tense. She wore a stylish black outfit that highlighted her graceful figure, adding an air of sophistication.

Her face showed concern, as though she had something important to share.

— Mr. Drake, Inspector Miller, — her voice trembled slightly as she stopped in front of them. — I have information that might help with your investigation.

Drake and Miller exchanged glances.

— What do you mean, Miss Harper? — Miller asked.

Amelia glanced nervously around, as if afraid someone might overhear.

— It's about Simon. The day before his death, I was in his office. We were discussing some financial documents, and I noticed he seemed troubled. He said he had suspicions — that someone in the family was plotting against him.

Edgar studied Amelia closely. Her tension was evident, but something about her behavior made him suspicious.

— What exactly did he tell you? — he asked, leaning in slightly.

Amelia averted her gaze, as though carefully choosing her words.

— He didn't say anything specific, — she replied. — Just mentioned that someone in the family might wish him harm. He had been very cautious lately, especially after Richard's death. It seemed to me that he had started distrusting everyone around him.

Miller scoffed.

— Distrusting everyone? Makes sense in a family where everyone's after the inheritance.

Amelia shook her head.

— No, it was more than that. He spoke about some records, documents that were supposed to surface soon. I don't know what they were, but he was certain they would cause a major scandal.

Edgar paused to consider this. If Simon had known something that could change the course of events or harm a family member, it could explain his murder.

— Miss Harper, do you know where these documents might be? — Edgar asked, fixing his gaze on her.

Amelia hesitated before answering.

— I'm not sure. But he kept something in his office. Perhaps those are the documents he mentioned.

Edgar exchanged a glance with Miller.

— We need to check Simon's office, — Miller said quietly but firmly.

Edgar nodded, but before they could move, Amelia spoke again.

— I… — she hesitated, clearly unsure if she should continue. — I noticed something else. When I was in his office that day, someone knocked on the door. I don't know who it was, but Simon seemed alarmed. He asked me to leave, saying he needed to talk to that person alone.

Edgar tensed.

— You didn't see who it was? — he asked.

Amelia shook her head again.

— No, I left as soon as he asked me to. But it felt wrong. I could sense something was off.

Miller frowned.

— And you didn't think to mention this sooner?

— I was scared, — Amelia admitted. — Everything happened so suddenly. First Richard's death, then Simon's... I didn't want anyone to suspect me of anything.

Edgar nodded thoughtfully.

— Your fears are understandable, Miss Harper. But if you remember anything else, don't hesitate to tell us.

Amelia nodded, and after a brief farewell, she hurried away, leaving Edgar and Miller alone.

— What do you think? — Miller asked once Amelia was out of sight.

Edgar sighed deeply.

— If Simon did have documents that could harm someone in the family, that could be the motive for his murder. We need to check his office immediately.

Miller nodded.

— I figured. Time to find out what this family is hiding.

Drake and Miller headed toward Simon's office, leaving behind yet another trail of unanswered questions. As they walked down the corridor, the mansion seemed unnaturally still, as if it was holding its breath. The corridors stretched endlessly, reminding them of the dark shadows that hung over this family. Both men were lost in their thoughts.

— If these documents really exist, they might shed light on everything, — Miller said, breaking the silence. — The question is, who knew about them?

Edgar nodded in silent agreement.

— Considering Amelia saw someone just before Simon's death, it seems that person knew more than the rest. Maybe that's our killer, — Edgar remarked as they reached the door to Simon's office.

The door was closed but unlocked. Edgar slowly turned the handle and carefully opened it. The room looked almost untouched since the initial police search, but there was no doubt that some things might have been overlooked.

Edgar glanced around. The office was spacious, with high ceilings and large windows that let in dim light. The walls were lined with paintings and shelves of books. In the center of the room stood a massive wooden desk — Simon's workspace and a potential hiding spot for important documents.

— Let's start with the desk, — Edgar said, pointing to the sturdy oak piece.

Miller nodded and began opening drawers. Each one held neatly arranged folders, documents, pens, and notebooks — everything seemed to be in its place.

— He was a meticulous man, — Miller noted, flipping through yet another folder.

Edgar moved to one of the cabinets and opened it. Inside was a stack of financial reports. He grabbed one folder and skimmed through it.

— These are standard financial documents. Everything looks clean, as if nothing ever happened, — he remarked.

However, something caught his attention: a small leather notebook tucked into the corner of one drawer. Edgar picked it up and opened it to the first page. The pages were filled with fine handwriting and numbers.

— Looks like Simon's personal notes, — he said, showing the notebook to Miller.

Miller leaned closer to take a look.

— Anything suspicious?

Edgar flipped through a few pages. Finally, on one page, a note caught his eye:

"RL documents — review next week. Confidential."

Edgar narrowed his eyes.

"It seems these are documents related to Richard Lancaster. Simon might have been planning to conduct a review or reveal something connected to his uncle's inheritance or business dealings."

Miller nodded.

"That might have been his leverage against someone. And perhaps that's what got him killed."

Edgar studied the notes intently before closing his notebook.

"We need to find out what these documents are and where they might be. They could be the key to everything."

They continued to search the office but found nothing else that could point them to the location of the documents. Drake and Miller left the office, aware that they were closer to solving the mystery but still far from the end.

"The next step is to talk to Andrew Lancaster," Edgar said. "I want to know what he knows about his father's documents and why Simon might have been interested in reviewing them."

Miller nodded in agreement.

"Time to get some answers."

Drake and Miller headed toward Andrew Lancaster's room, ready for what they anticipated would be a difficult conversation. However, as they approached the door, voices could be heard from inside. This was unexpected, as they hadn't thought Andrew would have company. Edgar gestured for Miller to stop, and they listened quietly.

"You don't understand!" a voice exclaimed irritably but muffled. "He must have found out about the documents. If he managed to make them public, it would ruin us."

Drake and Miller exchanged glances.

"Will you calm down already?" another voice replied, measured and cold. "Panic isn't going to solve anything."

Without hesitation, Edgar knocked on the door. Moments later, Andrew Lancaster opened it, his face tense despite his attempt to appear composed.

"Mr. Lancaster, we need to talk..." Edgar began but then noticed someone else in the room.

Standing in the corner, leaning against the wall, was Oliver Lancaster, Andrew's 19-year-old son from his first marriage. He was a tall young man with dark, nearly black short-cropped hair and deep brown eyes that carried a faint expression of disdain. His sharp cheekbones and reserved demeanor gave him the air of someone accustomed to hiding his emotions. Wearing a black sweater, he exuded a quiet, mysterious presence. Though he seemed aloof, his presence in the room was anything but incidental.

Andrew stepped aside, allowing Edgar and Miller to enter.

"It seems I interrupted an important discussion," Edgar remarked as he walked into the room.

Oliver glanced at him briefly before returning his gaze to the window, appearing indifferent to the situation.

"This is a family matter," Andrew said curtly, though his voice betrayed his unease.

Miller stepped closer to the desk, where scattered papers caught his attention.

"We've already determined that Simon was concerned about your father Richard's documents," Edgar said, looking at both Lancasters. "This seems to go beyond mere family affairs. What exactly were you discussing?"

Andrew pursed his lips, clearly struggling to maintain his composure.

"We were discussing the potential consequences if those documents were exposed," Andrew replied. "But it's just business matters. Oliver has nothing to do with this."

Oliver finally lifted his head, a sarcastic smirk curling his lips as he looked at his father.

"Business matters? If it weren't for your hesitation, we'd have resolved this issue long ago," he said coldly. "Now it's spiraling out of control."

Drake seized the moment of tension between father and son.

"Oliver," he addressed him directly, "we're aware of the conflicts you had with Simon, particularly regarding the family business. Did you accuse him of deceit?"

Oliver shrugged, his eyes flashing coldly.

"Simon was a liar. He spent his life scheming to take control of everything. I wasn't about to let him destroy what rightfully belonged to me."

Andrew shot an irritated glance at his son but said nothing.

"That's quite a serious accusation," Edgar noted. "How far were you willing to go to protect your inheritance?"

Oliver smirked, crossing his arms.

"If you're suggesting murder, Mr. Drake, you're mistaken. I didn't need to get my hands dirty. Simon destroyed himself with his greed and paranoia."

Edgar scrutinized Oliver, trying to determine if he was being truthful or merely deflecting suspicion. The room was thick with tension, and it seemed as though each of the Lancasters was hiding something.

"Perhaps," Edgar said. "But until we find those documents, everything remains uncertain. I trust you won't object if we conduct a more thorough search of your father's office?"

Oliver didn't respond, but a flicker of unease crossed his eyes.

Drake and Miller made their way back to Richard Lancaster's office. Though they had searched it earlier, new leads and growing suspicions compelled them to look again. Both felt the mounting tension. Oliver clearly had something to hide, and while he denied involvement in Simon's murder, his behavior suggested otherwise.

Once inside, Edgar went straight to the filing cabinets, while Miller examined the room, stopping near the desk.

"You know what bothers me?" Miller asked, looking at Edgar. "Everyone talks about these documents, but no one has said what's so important about them. The whole family dances around the subject without saying anything concrete."

Edgar nodded, continuing to sift through the shelves.

"Yes, it's troubling. Everyone seems to understand their significance, but no one wants to be direct about it. I suspect they contain more than just financial records. Perhaps something that could destroy the Lancasters' entire reputation."

Miller frowned in thought.

"And if Simon intended to expose it, he became a threat to them all. But who would be so afraid that they'd kill him?"

At that moment, Edgar found a small safe hidden in the corner of a cabinet. It was old, with a mechanical lock.

"This looks promising," Edgar said, tapping the metal surface.

Miller stepped closer, raising an eyebrow.

"Think the documents are in there?"

"Possibly," Edgar replied, examining the lock. "We need to figure out how to open it."

He studied the lock handle carefully but found no visible combination. Opening the safe without the code would be a challenge, but Edgar was certain the clue to unlocking it was nearby.

"We'll need to look for the code," he said, scanning the desk. "It might be hidden among the papers."

Miller nodded and began sifting through the documents on the desk. At that moment, the office door opened, and Geraldine Lancaster entered. Her face was pale, but her expression was resolute.

"I knew you'd be here," she began, her voice trembling slightly. "And I suspect you're looking for something that should have stayed within the family."

Edgar straightened, watching her intently.

"Mrs. Lancaster, do you know what might be in this safe?"

Geraldine stepped closer, her hands trembling slightly.

"I'm not sure what's inside," she said after a pause. "But I suspect those documents could destroy the entire Lancaster family. I'm not sure I want to know the truth."

Drake and Miller exchanged glances.

"We're here to uncover the truth, whatever it may be," Edgar said firmly. "If these documents are connected to Simon's death, we need to see them."

Geraldine hesitated, her face tense, before finally nodding. She stepped closer to Edgar and whispered,

"The combination is Richard's birth date."

Edgar raised an eyebrow in surprise. Geraldine gave a faint, humorless smile.

"You're a detective, Mr. Drake. I'm sure you've already figured that out," she said before leaving the room.

Edgar pondered her words, entered the combination he recalled from his research on Richard Lancaster, and slowly opened the safe.

Inside, neatly stacked folders immediately caught his eye. Their contents were far from ordinary financial reports or personal notes. The first pages revealed secrets of major deals involving members of the Lancaster family.

Miller stepped closer, his eyes widening as he scanned the names on the documents.

"It looks like we've found exactly what we were searching for," he said quietly.

Edgar nodded, quickly flipping through the pages.

"These records detail transactions that could be illegal. If Simon discovered this and planned to expose it, everyone in this house had a motive to stop him."

Suddenly, the study door opened again, and Oliver Lancaster stormed in. His face was tense, his eyes blazing as he spotted the documents in Edgar's hands.

"What are you doing?!" he shouted, rushing to the desk. "That's none of your business!"

Edgar remained calm, though his gaze was cold and piercing.

"It seems these aren't just financial records, Oliver. What were you trying to hide?"

Oliver froze for a moment, his fists clenching as his face hardened.

"These papers are meaningless!" he insisted, his tone tinged with desperation. "They're from the past—old affairs."

Miller stepped forward, blocking access to the documents.

"Maybe they're in the past for you, but it seems they could have been the reason your cousin lost his life."

Oliver glanced quickly at the door, as if considering making a run for it. But Edgar stepped closer.

"Who knew about these documents, Oliver? Who knew Simon might expose them?" Edgar's voice grew firmer.

Oliver flinched, his face contorting with tension.

"No one… no one was supposed to know. These were my father's dealings. Simon found out too much. He was going to ruin everything."

"And you decided to stop him?" Edgar asked quietly but sharply.

Oliver looked at Edgar, his eyes momentarily filled with despair, but then he abruptly turned away.

"I... I couldn't kill him. I wanted to silence him, but not like this."

A short, tense silence followed as all eyes focused on Oliver.

"Then who did?" Miller asked, his voice cutting through the air like ice.

At that moment, the door creaked open again, and Geraldine Lancaster stepped in. Her face was calm, but her eyes betrayed her concern.

"Oliver, stop," she said softly. "This isn't your fight anymore."

Oliver froze at the sound of her voice. His shoulders sagged, as if the weight of the situation had finally crushed him. He reluctantly turned to her, fear and despair evident in his eyes.

"You don't understand..." he murmured, stepping back. "Simon... he could have destroyed everything. I was trying to protect our name, to protect the family."

Geraldine moved into the room, her gaze steady as it locked onto Oliver.

"Protect the family?" she said, her tone calm but resolute. "You're too young to understand what real protection means. You've lost your way, Oliver. No one should have died for this."

Edgar observed the scene, feeling the tension in the room reach its peak.

"Mrs. Lancaster, what do you mean?" he asked, his voice measured but firm.

Geraldine hesitated for a moment before sighing.

"Oliver, do you really think this is all about business, about documents?" She shook her head. "It's not. Simon was a danger to all of us, not because of deals, but because he knew more than he should have."

Miller frowned, while Edgar took a step closer.

"And what did he know?" Edgar's voice was almost a whisper.

Geraldine turned to face him, her eyes gleaming with tension.

"Simon knew that Richard… wasn't who he seemed to be. He threatened to expose it, and he couldn't be stopped," she said, lowering her head as if lost in thought.

Oliver stood frozen, his face pale.

"What are you saying?" he asked, his voice trembling.

Geraldine looked at him with sorrow.

"Your family built everything on lies, Oliver. Simon wanted to tear it all down. And someone among us couldn't let that happen."

Edgar squinted slightly.

"Who exactly, Mrs. Lancaster?"

Before Geraldine could respond, the door burst open, and Andrew Lancaster stormed in. His face was pale, his eyes blazing with fury.

"You've gone too far, Geraldine!" he yelled, his voice cracking. "This isn't your place!"

Edgar quickly assessed the escalating situation.

"Mr. Lancaster, is there something you're hiding?" Edgar asked firmly, his eyes fixed on Andrew.

But before Andrew could answer, Geraldine turned to him sharply.

"It was you who killed Simon, wasn't it?" she said, her voice cold as steel. "You couldn't let him reveal everything. You were afraid of losing your inheritance."

Andrew froze, his eyes widening.

"You're insane!" he shouted. "That's a lie!"

The room fell into a charged silence. Andrew stood motionless, his face twisted with anger and panic. Geraldine stared at him with icy determination. Oliver, confused and overwhelmed, struggled to process what was unfolding, his breathing shallow.

"It's not a lie, Andrew," Geraldine said, her voice trembling but steady. "You knew that if Simon revealed the truth, it would ruin everything. Your power over this family would vanish. You were afraid of losing everything your father left you."

Andrew stepped forward, his eyes ablaze.

"I didn't kill Simon!" he shouted, though panic seeped into his voice. "I didn't want him to destroy everything, yes, but I didn't kill him!"

Edgar watched Andrew closely, sensing he was on the verge of breaking.

"Mr. Lancaster," Edgar said calmly but firmly, "if it wasn't you, then who? Who in your family would go so far to keep this hidden?"

Andrew glanced at Geraldine, then at Oliver. It felt as though the walls were closing in on him, trapping him. He opened his mouth to speak, but Oliver interrupted him.

"Father, you told me Simon was a threat," Oliver said softly, his voice tense. "You said something had to be done before he ruined everything. But you… you wouldn't go that far… would you?"

Andrew froze, his gaze unfocused.

"No…" he finally said, his voice barely audible.

Edgar stepped closer, his focus unwavering.

"Mr. Lancaster, it's best to tell the truth now," Edgar said. "Every moment of silence will cost you more than you realize."

Suddenly, Geraldine's voice broke the tense silence.

"He's not guilty," she said quietly but resolutely. All eyes turned to her.

Edgar frowned.

"What do you mean?" he asked, his voice tinged with anticipation.

Geraldine straightened, her expression cold and unreadable.

"Yes, I accused him, but he isn't guilty. We're all responsible for what happened," she said, her voice steady but filled with pain. "Everything that occurred is the result of the secrets we've kept from one another. But who struck the final blow—I don't know."

The room fell silent once more. Edgar realized Geraldine was trying to protect the family by refusing to incriminate anyone directly.

"Are you saying you don't know who did it?" Edgar clarified.

Geraldine nodded quietly.

"I know one thing: each of us, in some way, bears responsibility for what happened. But who killed Simon…" She hesitated. "That's still a question."

Miller, who had remained silent until now, stepped forward.

"Who was the last person to see Simon alive on the day of his death? Who was alone with him?" he asked sharply.

Andrew raised his gaze.

"It wasn't me. I only saw him that morning. And I wasn't alone with him."

Suddenly, Oliver raised his head, his face pale as he spoke in a barely audible voice:

"I saw Amelia. She was with him shortly before they found him dead."

Edgar watched Oliver intently as he quietly uttered Amelia's name. Everyone in the room froze, realizing that suspicion now fell on the late Richard Lancaster's personal assistant.

"Amelia?" Miller asked, eyeing Oliver skeptically. "Are you sure it was her?"

Oliver nodded, though his face was pale, and his voice weak.

"Yes, I saw her. She left the study just a few minutes before I went in. I heard their voices, but I couldn't make out what they were saying. And when I entered, Simon was already dead."

Andrew exhaled sharply, trying to process what he had just heard.

"It could have been her..." he muttered, but Edgar was not quick to draw conclusions.

"That's too simple," he finally said, addressing the group. "But we do need to speak with Amelia. At the very least, she might clarify some things."

Before they could move, a strange sound broke the silence—a distant thud, like a muffled explosion, echoed from outside the mansion. Everyone in the room tensed, exchanging uneasy glances.

"What was that?" Miller asked, his brow furrowing.

Without a word, Edgar moved to the window and peered out. The fog that enveloped the estate obscured much, but in the distance, along the path leading to the gates, a figure was visible.

"Someone's out there," Edgar said calmly, pointing toward the garden. "We need to find out what happened."

Chapter 2: Secrets Under the Veil of Mist

After the tense conversation in the study, Drake and Miller headed outside to investigate the strange noise that had echoed from the grounds. The fog blanketing the estate added a heavy, oppressive atmosphere. As they approached the pathway leading to the gates, they were confronted with an unexpected scene.

Peter Grace, the family economist, lay on the ground near the garden. His glasses were cracked, apparently shattered in the fall. He was curled on his side, his dark curly hair disheveled, and his eyes closed. Peter was a man of average height with a stocky build; his protruding stomach betrayed his struggle with weight that he had never quite managed to overcome. Blood stains were visible on his shirt, though at first glance, no wound could be seen. Beside him lay an empty bottle, as if it had fallen alongside him.

Miller quickly crouched down to check for a pulse.

"He's alive, but in critical condition," he announced, straightening. "It seems he was alone."

While Drake scanned the area, his eyes landed on a crumpled scrap of paper near Peter's body. Picking it up, he unfolded it carefully. The damp paper revealed a message, which he read aloud:

"Meet me at 8 PM under the old tree. Come alone."

Miller furrowed his brow as the words sank in.

"Eight o'clock?" he echoed, his gaze sharp on Drake. "That was exactly when we were all in the house."

Drake nodded, his mind already piecing together the details. At 8 PM, everyone—Drake, Miller, Geraldine, Oliver, and Andrew—had been in the study discussing Simon's death. None of them could have left the house to attend this meeting.

"This rules all of us out as suspects," Drake said, handing the note to Miller. "Someone else must have arranged to meet Peter."

Geraldine, watching the scene unfold, stepped forward, her expression anxious.

"Peter never mentioned he had a meeting," she said. "He'd been in the house all day."

Andrew scowled, his suspicion evident.

"If this note is real, then he planned to meet someone in secret. Someone lured him out here," he muttered.

Drake's sharp eyes caught faint footprints leading from Peter's body to the fence that enclosed the estate.

"We need to figure out who wrote this note and why Peter was here alone," he said quietly. "Whoever he was meeting didn't want us to find out."

Miller nodded, his expression focused.

"The bigger question is what he knew that made him a target. We need to find out who he planned to meet under that tree."

Before they could approach the tree, a figure emerged from the fog. It was Amelia Harper, Richard Lancaster's personal assistant. Her face was pale, her hair slightly disheveled, and she held a lantern, its light flickering weakly in the mist.

"What are you doing here?" Miller demanded sharply, his voice filled with suspicion.

Amelia met their eyes with a calm yet tense expression.

"I came to speak with Peter," she said evenly, though a trace of unease underlined her words. "I needed to talk to him about what he was planning to do."

Drake's eyes narrowed as he studied her.

"What exactly was he planning to do, and why does it matter so much?"

Amelia hesitated, her gaze briefly distant.

"It's about Simon," she said at last. "He discovered something… and it got him killed."

Drake's attention sharpened.

"What did Simon discover?" he asked, his tone firm but measured.

Amelia took a deep breath, as if steeling herself.

"He uncovered details about Richard Lancaster's dealings," she admitted. "Transactions that could ruin everything. When Simon started digging through the records, he realized something was wrong with the company. Peter knew more about it than anyone. Once Simon started gathering evidence, he became a threat to everyone involved."

Miller, standing nearby, frowned deeply.

"So Peter knew about these deals?"

Amelia nodded.

"Yes. As the chief economist, he had access to all the financial documents. But Peter was cautious; he knew this information could destroy not just his career but his life. After Simon's death, Peter realized he couldn't stay silent anymore."

"And you were supposed to meet him here?" Drake clarified.

"Yes," Amelia admitted. "He said he'd found something important and wanted to tell me everything. We agreed to meet here. But someone got to him first."

Drake and Miller exchanged a look, realizing Peter might not be the only one with knowledge of the truth. Despite his critical condition, Peter was still alive.

"Miller, call for medical assistance immediately," Drake ordered, shifting into action. "Peter has to survive. He may be our only chance to uncover what's going on."

Miller nodded and quickly pulled out his phone, dialing for an ambulance.

Amelia continued speaking, her voice trembling slightly.

"I came alone, just as he asked. I waited, but when I found him lying here... I thought I was too late."

"He's still alive, and we'll do everything we can to keep him that way," Drake assured her firmly. Checking Peter again, he noticed the faintest movement—his fingers twitching slightly.

Minutes later, the wail of ambulance sirens cut through the night's eerie silence. Paramedics arrived promptly, administering first aid and preparing Peter for transport.

Turning to Amelia, Drake posed one last question.

"What exactly was he planning to tell you? Do you have any idea what it was?"

Amelia shook her head.

"He only said it was about Richard's documents. If he revealed them, the truth would come out, and the family would never be the same."

Drake nodded grimly, watching as the medics loaded Peter into the ambulance.

"We'll look into those documents. But someone has already tried to take Peter out of the picture. We need to find out who they are and why they're so desperate to hide the truth."

As the ambulance disappeared through the gates, the night once again enveloped the estate in heavy silence. Miller paced nervously along the pathway, his steps quick and sharp.

"What now?" he asked irritably. "Peter is barely alive. Even if he wakes up, we don't know if he'll be able to tell us anything."

Drake, lost in thought, gazed at the house shrouded in fog.

"We need to study those documents," he said softly. "If Peter really knew something crucial, it could be the key to solving this mystery."

Edgar nodded, though his gaze remained fixed on the garden where the recent events had unfolded. Dozens of thoughts raced through his mind. Someone was determined to ensure Peter remained silent. And that someone was likely still inside the mansion.

"Amelia," Edgar addressed her as they re-entered the house, "do you know where the documents Peter mentioned are kept?"

She nodded slightly, her face still pale.

"Yes. They should be in the safe in Richard's study. But I'm not sure if I have access. Only Richard and his lawyer, Martin Hudson, had full rights to those papers."

Miller squinted.

"Then the next person we need to speak to is Martin Hudson."

Edgar nodded, recognizing that the lawyer could hold the key to unlocking the family's secrets.

"We'll meet with him tomorrow," Edgar said. "But for now, Amelia, we need your cooperation. If you have any access to the documents, even partial, it could help us start piecing this together."

Amelia nodded silently and headed toward the study, with Drake and Miller following her.

When they entered Richard's study, the atmosphere was tense. Edgar scanned the room, his eyes settling on the heavy desk and the shelves brimming with files. Amelia approached a cabinet, running her finger along the metallic lock on one of the drawers.

"Here," she said, her voice trembling. "But I don't know the code."

"We can try to open it later," Edgar said, examining the lock.

At that moment, a faint sound—a barely audible rustling—caught his attention. Without a word, he signaled to Miller and moved cautiously to the door, opening it abruptly.

The hallway was empty, but fresh footprints marked the floor. They were still damp from the morning dew, clearly made recently. Edgar frowned.

"It seems someone was watching us."

Miller crouched to examine the prints closely. They led deeper into the hallway, disappearing into the mansion's shadows. He looked up at Edgar, their unspoken thought shared in a glance.

"Someone is definitely keeping an eye on us. And that someone doesn't want us to find those documents," Miller murmured.

Edgar narrowed his eyes, his mind already working through possible scenarios. Turning to Amelia, who stood silently in the corner, he asked,

"The safe isn't the only target. Someone in this house is trying to monitor our every move. Can you think of anyone else who might know about the documents? Has anyone shown unusual interest in Richard's affairs recently?"

Amelia hesitated, her face growing even paler.

"I… I'm not sure," she said softly. "But… Evelyn spent a lot of time in Richard's study after his death. Maybe she knows something she hasn't told us."

Edgar nodded, filing away the information. Evelyn, Richard's widow, had seemed cold and distant from the start. But what if she was hiding more than her grief?

"We'll speak to Evelyn tomorrow morning," Edgar said. "But for now, we need to search the rest of the house. We have to find out who's been following us."

Miller agreed, and they decided to follow the corridors, tracking the footprints to see where they led.

Drake and Miller's steps echoed softly in the mansion's long hallways. In the dim light of the old lamps, shadows around them seemed to grow darker and more menacing. The farther they went, the fainter the footprints became, eventually blending into the carpet.

Suddenly, Miller stopped abruptly, straining to listen. A faint noise—like a door opening or something heavy being moved—came from another part of the house. Edgar gave a silent nod, and they moved toward the sound.

Reaching the door to one of the farthest rooms, Edgar opened it cautiously. The room was dimly lit but appeared to be recently used.

A book with marked pages lay on the desk. Miller picked it up, skimming the notes scribbled in the margins. They were clippings from old articles related to Richard Lancaster's dealings, including mentions of financial scandals and possible lawsuits.

Edgar's eyes scanned the room, landing on a door leading to the terrace. It was slightly ajar.

"It looks like someone left through here," he said, pointing to footprints leading outside. "We might be close."

Drake and Miller stepped out onto the terrace. The cool night air hit their faces as thick fog crept along the ground like a veil. The tracks in the damp grass led around the side of the mansion, disappearing into the mist.

"Let's see where this takes us," Edgar murmured, bending down to study the trail more closely.

They moved along the wall of the mansion, ears attuned to every sound around them. The fog muffled their footsteps, amplifying the eerie silence.

Turning the corner of the building, they came upon a small, secluded clearing hidden from the mansion's main entrance. Near an old tree stood a figure with its back to them.

Miller gestured toward the figure, and Edgar nodded silently. They approached cautiously.

"Who's there?" Edgar's sharp voice cut through the night.

The figure flinched and turned. It was Martin Hudson, the family's lawyer. His face was tense, his hands trembling.

"What are you doing out here at this hour?" Miller added, stepping forward.

Martin stared at them in surprise, as though he hadn't expected to be caught.

"I… I just needed some fresh air," he began, his voice shaky. "This situation with Peter… and everything else…" His words trailed off.

Edgar watched him intently, doubting every word.

"Fresh air? At three in the morning, near the back of the mansion?" Edgar's tone was skeptical. "That doesn't sound convincing, Martin."

Miller crossed his arms, narrowing his eyes.

"We heard noises back here. Were you trying to eavesdrop or follow us?"

Martin paled, hesitating as his eyes darted around, seemingly searching for an escape.

"I… I was worried about the documents," he finally admitted, his voice gaining a hint of steadiness. "I knew Peter might have done something with Richard's papers, so I wanted to check the safe."

Edgar took a step closer.

"Or were you trying to hide something?" he asked, his piercing gaze fixed on Martin's eyes.

The lawyer stiffened, his face growing even paler.

"No! I'm not hiding anything! I just wanted to make sure everything was in order," he replied, his voice defensive.

Miller stepped back, scrutinizing Martin from head to toe.

"We're not detaining you yet, but you'd better be prepared for a serious conversation tomorrow. Your connection to this case is becoming harder to ignore."

Martin nodded, his gaze falling to the ground. He seemed overwhelmed, fully aware that his actions only raised more suspicion.

Chapter 3: Morning Reveals Its Secrets

The mansion was enveloped in silence that felt even thicker than at night. Drake and Miller arrived at Richard's office early in the morning, determined to finally open the safe Amelia had mentioned. But when they approached the massive desk and opened the safe door, they were met with an unpleasant surprise: the safe was ajar, and its contents were missing.

Miller frowned, looking over the empty safe.

"Seems someone got here before us," he said grimly.

Edgar, folding his arms, surveyed the office. There were no signs of forced entry, and the safe's lock was undamaged. Whoever had done this clearly knew the combination and had opened the safe easily, as if they were at home.

"The question is, who could have done this and what exactly were they looking for," Edgar said quietly. "And, even more importantly—how did they manage to get past us?"

They searched the office again for clues but found nothing indicating who might have been there before their arrival. The only hint was the missing documents and… faint fingerprints on a dusty shelf near the safe. The prints were blurred, as if someone had deliberately tried to hide them but had still left a slight trace.

Miller carefully gathered the prints from the shelf, planning to have them analyzed later.

"This clearly wasn't an accident," Miller noted. "We're almost certain Martin Hudson was interested in the documents. Perhaps he's the one who took them."

Edgar frowned, realizing the situation was growing more tense.

"He wouldn't have dared to act alone," Edgar said. "Someone may have helped him. He has connections, and possibly someone in the house knew what he was planning."

At that moment, Evelyn Lancaster, Richard's widow, entered the office. She shot them a piercing glance, her face cold, though there was anxiety in her eyes.

"Is there something I can help with?" she asked evenly, though she seemed slightly on edge.

Edgar looked at her, keeping his suspicions hidden.

"We were hoping to speak with you about some of Richard's documents," he said calmly. "They disappeared from the safe last night. We'd like to know if you're aware of what was in them."

Evelyn tilted her head, her face remaining expressionless.

"I have nothing to do with Richard's affairs," she said. "Since his death, I rarely come to this office. I thought all family matters had been entrusted to his lawyer, Martin Hudson."

Miller noticed a flicker of unease on her face, though she was trying hard to conceal it.

"But did you know that Martin was here last night?" Miller asked. "He seemed very interested in those papers."

Evelyn sighed shortly, narrowing her eyes as if carefully considering her response.

"Martin was always far too invested in Richard's affairs, even after his death," she replied dryly. "Perhaps you should ask him if you want to know more."

At that moment, the doorbell rang, and Amelia appeared at the office door.

"Sorry to interrupt, but there's an inspector with a report from the hospital. He wants to speak to you about Peter's condition."

Edgar exchanged glances with Miller. Perhaps Peter's condition could shed light on what had happened. Leaving the office, they headed to the inspector, sensing that this new turn in the case would be tied to the missing documents and the strange night when someone had managed to bypass their plans.

Drake and Miller went into the hall, where the inspector with the hospital report was waiting for them. He was a tall, middle-aged man with a tired face. He gave them a restrained nod and handed over a folder.

"Peter survived," the inspector began, "but his condition remains unstable. He hasn't regained consciousness yet, but... our doctors found something interesting."

Drake and Miller exchanged quick glances.

"What exactly?" Edgar asked cautiously.

The inspector opened the folder, showing them pages of medical records.

"There were traces of a substance similar to a tranquilizer found in his blood. It seems someone deliberately tried to knock him out before inflicting the injuries. Whoever did this likely wanted to make sure he wouldn't be able to tell anyone anything."

Miller frowned, studying the report.

"So someone clearly made sure Peter couldn't talk. This same person may have emptied the safe."

Edgar nodded, deep in thought. If Peter had been drugged before the attack, it meant the culprit had planned carefully and was likely well-acquainted with the house and its residents.

"Do you have any information on how Peter received the substance? Could he have drunk something before the meeting?"

The inspector shook his head.

"At this point, we can't say for sure. But we did find a small injection mark on his arm. The drug was likely administered shortly before he was found."

Miller and Edgar silently processed the new information. This opened up a new line of investigation: someone close to Peter not only threatened him but may have planned to permanently remove him from the picture, acting discreetly and with calculation.

Suddenly, Amelia entered the hall with a worried expression.

"Sorry to interrupt, but I found this on the desk in the office. It might be important," she said, handing them a small envelope with a letter addressed to Richard Lancaster.

Edgar carefully opened the envelope. Inside was a short note, written in neat handwriting:

"If the truth comes out, your secrets will fall with your legacy. I have everything under control."

There was no signature, but a single initial "M" was at the bottom.

Miller narrowed his eyes.

"'M'... Whoever this is clearly threatened Richard even while he was alive. Richard may have been trying to hide something, and after his death, this burden passed on to Peter."

Edgar carefully put the note back into the envelope.

"We need to find out who this 'M' is and what secret Richard kept locked away," he said. "And find out why it's now a threat to everyone living here."

Drake and Miller looked once more at the empty safe. A dark suspicion flashed through Edgar's mind: if Richard Lancaster had really been hiding important secrets, then the missing documents might contain crucial evidence.

Amelia carefully entered the office behind them.

"Sorry, but I think something has been overlooked," she said quietly. "Richard often used the safe not only for documents but to store personal items he kept close."

Miller looked at her with interest.

"You mean there were things in there besides papers?"

She nodded.

"Yes, among other things, he kept family jewelry, several old letters, and…" she hesitated, choosing her words, "something like a ring. Richard called it 'the key to his future.' I saw it only once—Richard quickly put the ring back in the safe, but he said it held special meaning."

Edgar frowned.

"A ring? And something tied to it?"

Amelia shrugged, but her gaze showed uncertainty.

"Maybe it was just jewelry, but Richard treated it as a symbol. He said that after his death, the ring should go to a family member who would earn that trust. But I don't know who he intended it for."

At that moment, Oliver Lancaster, Richard's grandson and Andrew's son, appeared in the doorway of the office. His face showed concern.

"Sorry, I overheard your conversation. If this is about the ring my grandfather Richard kept, he once told me about it. He called the ring a 'symbol of trust' and said it was meant for someone who would keep the family together. But it sounded strange. Do any of you know what he meant?"

Edgar exchanged glances with Amelia and Miller.

"Seems Richard created a series of riddles he wanted to leave as a legacy," Edgar said. "But if the ring, this 'symbol of trust,' is missing along with the documents, this may mean someone doesn't want the family to learn their true meaning."

Amelia looked confused.

"Maybe the answer is somewhere in his letters or documents. He always treated family, business, and inheritance as a chain of secrets where answers could only be found by knowing key details."

Oliver looked thoughtful.

"If the ring was as important as he said," he said, "then maybe it was hidden somewhere in the house so that the person meant to find it could do so."

Edgar frowned.

"We need to find out more about the ring and its meaning, as well as determine who else might have known about it. This may explain why the documents disappeared and why Peter was attacked."

Miller nodded.

"We're due for a serious talk with Martin Hudson—he might know why this ring was so important."

As soon as Oliver left, Edgar looked thoughtfully at Miller.

"We need to speak with Martin Hudson as soon as possible. He's clearly tied to the disappearance of the documents and possibly to this ring," Edgar said. "If this ring was so important to Richard, Martin might have the most to gain from its disappearance."

Miller nodded, his expression serious.

"I'll contact Hudson and ask him to come here immediately," he said, heading to make the call.

A few hours later, Martin Hudson arrived at the mansion. His face was cautious, but as always, he kept a composed demeanor. He entered the office where Drake and Miller were waiting.

Edgar didn't waste any time.

"Mr. Hudson, we need to talk about the ring Richard Lancaster called 'the key to his future.' We've learned that you were one of the few people he ever showed it to. Do you know where it is now?"

Martin paused, his face slightly pale.

"I did know about the ring, but I was told it would stay in the family. I never thought it would disappear. To be honest, I don't know where it could be."

Miller narrowed his eyes, studying Martin's expression closely.

"In that case, how do you explain the disappearance of documents from the safe? We know you were interested in Richard's papers and were seen near the mansion last night."

Martin looked flustered for a moment but quickly composed himself.

"I was simply doing my duty. Richard's affairs were never straightforward, and after his death, some of the responsibilities fell to me. If I searched the safe, it was only for the family's benefit." His voice was sharp, though there was a faint nervousness in his gaze.

Edgar stepped closer.

"We found a note with the initial 'M' among Richard's papers. Perhaps you know what this 'control' it mentions refers to? The note said his secrets would ruin his legacy."

Martin's face turned pale. He lowered his gaze, his hands shaking.

"Richard was... a man of many secrets. He hid his past, and some things in his affairs always raised questions. We worked together for many years, and... maybe some of his plans went beyond the law. But I never interfered. My job was to protect him and his family, not control them."

Miller stepped forward.

"But now everything is at stake. The documents are missing, the ring is gone, and Peter is in the hospital because he knew too much. You need to tell us what you really know."

Martin swallowed nervously and nodded.

"Richard used the ring not just as a symbol. It was the key to certain… bank accounts and important legal documents. Whoever held it would have access to resources known only to a select few. I wasn't supposed to reveal this, but now that things have gone this far… I'm afraid someone in the family has decided to take advantage of this secret for personal gain."

Drake and Miller exchanged glances.

"This ring might be why someone's willing to do anything to secure the inheritance," Edgar said quietly. "If one of the family members already knows about this, the ring has become a dangerous asset."

Miller nodded.

"In that case, Mr. Hudson, stay at the mansion. We don't want anyone leaving the premises until the investigation is finished."

Martin nodded, his face full of despair. He understood that the situation was becoming more serious and that his own past with Richard now threatened the entire Lancaster legacy.

After talking with Andrew and Lucy, Drake and Miller headed to the library where Richard often spent his evenings. On one of the shelves, Edgar noticed an old photo album with a worn cover. Flipping through its pages, they came across an old photograph of a young Richard with an unfamiliar man. On the back, there was a handwritten note: "Our day will come soon," and at the bottom, the initials "M.H."

Miller looked at Edgar in surprise.

"This could be Martin Hudson," he said. "But why were they working together long before the family business was even created?"

Edgar frowned, studying the note.

"Maybe it's an old promise or a commitment that keeps Martin protecting the family's secrets."

Their thoughts were interrupted by a quiet rustling outside the door. They turned sharply, but the corridor was empty. A shadow had just disappeared around the corner, leaving them puzzled. They realized that finding the photo album might have drawn unwanted attention—someone was clearly watching their movements and wanted to hide the truth.

Drake and Miller, having returned to the library after inspecting the corridor, focused again on the album of photographs. Both were deep in thought about the unidentified man in the old photo with Richard.

"That third person," Edgar said thoughtfully, studying the photograph, "his face is hidden in shadow, but it seems he wasn't just an incidental acquaintance. Maybe he's connected to the secrets Richard was so intent on keeping."

Miller nodded.

"If Martin really had longstanding ties with Richard, then this person likely played a role, too. They could have been involved in something together, even before Richard built his business."

Their thoughts were interrupted by the sound of footsteps—Evelyn, Richard's widow, entered the library. She noticed the photograph in Edgar's hands and stopped for a moment, her expression becoming cautious.

"These are old photos," she said slowly, then came closer, as if to take a better look at the picture. "Richard... he rarely spoke of that time."

Edgar looked at her intently.

"Do you recognize this man in the photo?" he asked, pointing to the barely visible figure next to Richard and the unknown man.

Evelyn turned her gaze away, her fingers nervously fidgeting with the hem of her dress.

"I can't say for sure... but I think I saw him once. It was before we married. Richard never explained who this man was, but he said he was connected to his 'hardest decisions.'"

Miller and Edgar exchanged glances. This information was hard to ignore—the figure in the photo could point to deep secrets in Richard's life that even his family didn't know about.

Edgar closed the album and said quietly:

"I think we need to find Martin. He may be able to shed some light on Richard's past and his old connections."

Evelyn looked at them, her eyes reflecting anxiety.

"Be careful with this," she warned. "If Richard's past is really coming back, it could destroy everything he built."

Drake and Miller decided to find Martin Hudson immediately. Edgar realized that their next step was to uncover more about Richard's past and the mysterious man in the photo. They walked down the dark corridor toward the office where Martin usually stayed to work when he visited the mansion.

When they reached the office door, it was locked.

"He's locked himself in, even though he knew we were coming to talk to him," Miller frowned, glancing at Edgar. "That's suspicious."

Edgar knocked on the door.

"Martin, it's Drake. We need to discuss something important."

There was no response. They exchanged glances, and Miller suggested breaking in, but at that moment, they heard a faint sound from inside. Someone quickly approached the door and unlocked it.

The door opened slightly, and Martin, clearly flustered, peered out.

"Sorry, I didn't mean to delay you," he said hastily. "I was sorting through Richard's affairs."

Edgar stepped inside, carefully observing the lawyer.

"We've learned that Richard had longstanding ties with a certain person who may still be a threat to the family," he said bluntly. "Were you aware of this?"

Martin took a step back, his face tense.

"I… can't explain everything," he replied cautiously. "I'll only say that Richard made several deals that required serious commitments. This person," Martin paused, choosing his words, "was one of those people Richard preferred to keep at a distance."

Miller stepped forward, his voice cold.

"So why didn't he tell anyone in the family?"

Martin looked down at the floor.

"Because the family's legacy was at stake. This person... he had influence, and Richard was willing to go to great lengths to keep the truth hidden."

Edgar studied Martin, assessing his words.

"If that's true, then he can still influence the Lancasters. I believe if we find this person, we'll have answers to all our questions."

Martin sighed and slowly nodded.

"I never knew his real name, only his initial—M," he said quietly. "Perhaps someone from Richard's circle can help you further. That's all I can say."

As Drake and Miller left Martin's office, the atmosphere in the mansion felt even more tense. They were heading toward the main hall when Lucy approached them. Her expression showed she wanted to say something but was hesitating.

"I need to talk to you," she said quietly, glancing around as if she was afraid of being overheard. "It's about my father's past."

Edgar nodded, and the three of them went into a small sitting room. After closing the door behind them, Lucy began to speak.

"I never mentioned this because my father forbade it," she began. "He sometimes received letters from a man he called an 'old friend.'

But whenever I asked, he would sharply dismiss me, saying it was personal."

Miller narrowed his eyes.

"Did you ever see those letters?"

Lucy shook her head.

"No. But once, I accidentally overheard part of their conversation. It was in my father's old office in London. They were talking about some 'deal' that was supposed to 'stay in the past.' But I don't know what they meant. It was long ago, and when my father realized I'd heard, he immediately changed the subject."

Drake and Miller exchanged glances. Lucy pointed to a cabinet in the corner of the room.

"After his death, I went through his old documents. I didn't find any of those letters, but there's a drawer in that cabinet that I was never able to open. There might be something important in there," she added.

Edgar walked over to the cabinet, which looked large and antique, with a small locked drawer. Lucy handed him a key that hadn't been used in a long time.

"Try this," she offered.

When Edgar turned the key, the drawer opened with a faint click. Inside lay a small bundle of old letters tied with a faded ribbon. Each one was marked "Personal. Do not send."

Edgar slowly untied the ribbon and opened the first letter. It was handwritten:

"You made your choice, Richard. There's no going back. Time has taken much, but the debt remains. If you decide to break our agreement, the consequences will be severe for all of us."

There was no signature, but at the bottom was a single mark—the letter "M."

Miller looked at Edgar intently.

"It seems this person still has power over the family, even after Richard's death."

Lucy paled upon hearing the message.

"Do you think he's returned? That he… is threatening us now?"

Edgar looked at her thoughtfully.

"Until we find this man, your family is at risk. It seems Richard's old debts are far more serious than anyone could have imagined."

Chapter 4: An Evening of Secrets

At dinner, Drake and Miller gathered all the mansion's residents in the grand but somber dining room. Present were everyone in the house who might know something about Richard Lancaster's past: Evelyn, the late Richard's widow; Andrew and Lucy, his children; Oliver, his grandson; Geraldine, Simon's former wife; Amelia, Richard's personal assistant; and Martin Hudson, the family's lawyer.

Each took their place at the long table, and the tension was almost palpable. Edgar glanced at everyone before beginning.

"We've gathered you to discuss the identity of someone Richard Lancaster referred to as his 'old friend.' However, according to our information, he was no friend in the usual sense of the word," he said calmly.

Silence hung over the table until Andrew finally spoke, his face pensive.

"My father was always a secretive man. He kept his affairs to himself, even if they affected the family. If this person was a friend, why did he never appear among us?"

Lucy glanced at her mother, who sat across from her, and quietly added:

"I remember once my father mentioned him, but he spoke as though he was forced to maintain this connection. I'd never seen him so tense after one of their talks."

Evelyn looked at Edgar, hesitating slightly before speaking.

"Perhaps I did see him once," she said cautiously, her voice subdued. "It was early in our marriage. Richard told me that this man could be dangerous for our family, and he asked me to keep silent about him."

Edgar listened intently as Martin began to speak.

"This person, as I understand, was a partner of Richard's even before the family reached its current status," he said, lowering his voice slightly. "Perhaps he was involved in building the business, but over time his role grew darker. And when Richard realized he had gone too far, there was no turning back."

The discussion was interrupted when Amelia suddenly rose from the table.

"Excuse me, I need to step out for a moment," she said, and without waiting for a response, left the dining room.

No sooner had she left than a loud thud echoed from the corridor, startling everyone. Drake and Miller jumped up and hurried to the door, stepping into the hallway. There they found Amelia, lying unconscious on the floor beside a broken vase.

"What happened?!" Lucy cried in panic.

Edgar checked Amelia's pulse and felt a faint beat. Meanwhile, Miller noticed the broken vase and faint marks trailing along the carpet. He frowned as he examined the shards.

"This doesn't seem accidental," he said quietly to Edgar. "The vase might have been meant for someone else. But who could have known that Amelia would be the one to step out?"

Edgar paused, thinking.

"This looks like a warning, but for whom? If M has an accomplice here, then everyone in this house is in danger."

After Drake and Miller examined the scene, medics arrived at the house. Amelia was still unconscious, and they took her to the hospital to be kept under observation. As she was carried out on a stretcher, the family members exchanged anxious glances, each trying to hide their growing tension.

Edgar looked at Miller.

"Something tells me this wasn't just an accident," he said. "Maybe someone in the house is testing us, playing with our attention."

When Amelia arrived at the same hospital where Peter was staying, Drake and Miller planned to visit her in the morning. However, early that morning, Edgar received an unexpected call from the hospital: Peter, whose condition had seemed stable, had suddenly passed away, and the circumstances of his death were suspicious.

In the hospital corridor, Edgar was met by the doctor, whose face showed confusion and concern.

"We regret to inform you that, despite a successful recovery, there was a sudden crisis last night, and we were unable to save him," the doctor said quietly. "It was unexpected—his test results had shown improvement, and we were preparing him for discharge."

Edgar pressed his lips together, realizing that Peter's sudden death might not be a mere coincidence.

"Are there any clues that indicate the cause of this crisis?" he asked.

The doctor frowned and sighed.

"It seems that traces of a substance, possibly a tranquilizer, were found in his system, but in much higher concentration than usual. We are running tests to confirm this."

When Edgar returned to the mansion and shared the news with Miller and the rest, the atmosphere grew even more strained.

Everyone present now sensed that danger was lurking closer than ever.

Evelyn paled upon hearing the news about Peter.

"This has gone too far. If Peter… if he was murdered, who will be next?"

Miller surveyed those gathered with a dark look.

"Someone wants to scare you all—or force you to keep quiet. We need to find out what Peter knew and why he became a target."

After the incident with the vase, Amelia was taken to the hospital for examination. The next day, when her condition was deemed stable, she returned to the mansion—tired, but determined to help clarify the situation. Following her return, Drake and Miller decided to question each of the household members to gather information about Richard Lancaster's mysterious past and try to understand who might be behind the threats.

First, they gathered everyone in the library. Edgar stood, glanced around at those gathered, and announced:

"Over the past few days, several serious incidents have occurred, including the sudden death of Peter. We now have sufficient reason to believe this is connected to obligations left by Richard Lancaster.

We'll speak with each of you to understand what you may know about Richard's affairs and his 'old friend.'"

Evelyn was the first to remain for questioning. Sitting across from Edgar, she tried to hide her anxiety, but her hands trembled slightly.

"Mrs. Lancaster," Edgar began, "do you know of any of your husband's affairs that could harm the family?"

Evelyn looked away, then spoke quietly:

"Richard rarely shared his affairs with me, especially if they troubled him. But once, I overheard him speaking with a certain man. There was fear in his voice, as if... as if he was forced to maintain the relationship, though he had long wanted to end it."

Edgar noted her words thoughtfully.

When Evelyn left, Andrew entered. Tension was evident in his gaze.

"I knew my father had certain obligations," he said, leaning back in his chair. "But he avoided talking about them. I think he was tied to this man somehow, but feared it would affect us badly. It seemed like a secret he preferred to take to his grave."

Then Edgar called in Amelia, who had recently returned from the hospital. She looked tired but firmly took her seat across from Drake and Miller.

"Richard rarely opened up to anyone, but I had to know more because of my work with his documents," she admitted. "In recent months, he asked me to keep an eye on his papers. There were reports, financial data, and some papers he trusted me to hide."

Miller frowned.

"What kinds of papers? Why didn't he trust them with his family or his lawyer?"

Amelia sighed, glancing at those present.

"I don't know the details. But some of those reports included names and companies that were never mentioned in official business. I think he feared his secrets would come to light," her voice trembled, "but someone has clearly figured out where to look."

Drake and Miller exchanged glances, realizing they were closer to an answer: Richard's past held more threats than they had anticipated, and that past was beginning to affect the entire family.

After Drake and Miller questioned all the family members, it became clear that these interviews didn't bring much clarity to the case. It seemed that each person was either hiding something, or they truly knew little about Richard's connections and mysterious past. This realization only heightened the tension.

They returned to the library, going over the information they had gathered, when a loud noise came from the far wing of the mansion. Drake and Miller immediately rushed towards the sound and soon found themselves at the door of one of the parlors. Inside, they found Lucy, standing in front of a broken window, looking around in confusion.

"I heard a noise and came to see what happened," she explained in a shaky voice, barely able to stand. "I thought someone was breaking in…"

Miller examined the scene and noted that there were no tracks by the window, yet shards of broken glass and scraps of fabric were scattered on the floor as if someone had brushed against the window frame.

"Looks like someone was trying to scare us," said Miller, inspecting the traces. "But if this person was inside, why did no one see them?"

Edgar sighed, realizing that the situation was growing even more confusing.

"We're reaching a point where it's obvious that someone is watching each of you. Someone may be observing your every move."

He turned to Lucy, who looked pale.

"Perhaps Richard left something for you that could help reveal the truth?"

She nodded, trying to pull herself together.

"Yes… in his study, there are several old photographs and a box he never let me open. Maybe there's something there that explains why we've all become targets."

When she entered the study with Miller and Lucy, Edgar noticed a safe hidden behind a painting. The safe had a lock, which, according to Lucy, had always seemed especially important to her father.

After a few moments of thought, Edgar picked the lock and opened the safe. Inside was a small box, tied with an old ribbon. Attached to the box was a note that read, "Do not open until after my death."

Inside, they found photographs of Richard with the same unknown man they had heard about, as well as another familiar figure.

Inside the box, they found several photographs. In one of them, Richard stood beside the unknown man the family members had described before: his face was resolute, his features sharp. The third person in the photo turned out to be Martin Hudson, the family's lawyer. This discovery suggested that Martin was not just a legal advisor, but likely a close partner of Richard in the past.

As Drake and Miller examined the photographs, Martin himself entered the study. Catching sight of the photos, he froze, his face momentarily showing tension before he quickly composed himself.

"You've already learned a lot," he said quietly, looking at the photo. "I think it's time I tell you the full story."

Edgar gestured for him to sit, and Martin, sighing heavily, settled into a chair.

"Richard and I knew each other long before he established the family business," he began, avoiding his companions' gaze. "There were things no one was ever supposed to know. Richard wanted to secure a prosperous future for his family, but behind it lay a connection to one man—Maxwell Hunt."

Drake and Miller exchanged glances upon hearing the name.

"Who is Maxwell Hunt?" Edgar asked calmly.

Martin paused briefly before responding:

"He was our partner, a man willing to do anything for his own gain. Richard thought he could keep him under control, but that proved impossible. After one major deal, Maxwell disappeared, but Richard always believed he'd return sooner or later."

Miller frowned.

"Are you saying this man now threatens the family?"

Martin nodded slowly.

"Richard warned me many times that if he were ever gone, Maxwell might come for what he considers his share. It's possible he's nearby even now, ready to finish what he started."

Edgar paused briefly, considering what he'd just heard.

"So your 'partner' is willing to take any steps to claim what he wants," he said, studying Martin's face. "The question is, how far is he willing to go?"

Martin said nothing, but his silence and tense gaze spoke volumes.

After the tense conversation with Martin, it became clear: if Maxwell Hunt had indeed returned, his goal was to gain control over the family assets and achieve his aims at any cost. Edgar understood that there was little time for discussion; action was needed.

"Martin," he said, "we need to check Richard's study. If you have any information or papers that could shed light on what we're looking for, I suggest you show us right now."

Martin nodded, and together with Miller, they headed to Richard's study, hoping to find at least some tangible clue. When Edgar opened the doors, he saw that the study was immaculate—as if Richard himself were still guarding it from prying eyes.

Edgar began to inspect the desk, checking drawers and cabinets. Within a few minutes, they discovered a hidden compartment in the desk. Opening it, Edgar found an old file of documents. It contained financial reports and contracts signed by both Richard and Maxwell Hunt. One of the documents outlined a substantial financial obligation, with a clause stating that Maxwell held a share in certain key assets of the Lancaster family.

Miller frowned, carefully studying the papers.

"It seems Maxwell not only had influence over family affairs but also the right to claim his part," he said. "This is likely what he's come back for now that Richard is no longer here to oppose him."

Edgar nodded.

"That explains his return. He's waiting for the family to either agree to his terms—or he'll start removing anyone who stands in his way."

Chapter 5: Hidden Past

After discovering the documents confirming Maxwell Hunt's claim to a share of the Lancaster family assets, Edgar understood that in order to uncover the truth, he needed to meet this man face-to-face. Martin, who knew Maxwell, offered to help arrange the meeting, knowing that there was no other way.

Edgar decided to invite Maxwell to the mansion and personally question him about his connections to the family and his interests that might threaten the Lancasters. The anticipation leading up to the meeting was intense; everyone in the house felt that Hunt's arrival could bring new challenges, but it was the only way to reveal his true intentions.

The next day, Maxwell Hunt arrived at the mansion. He turned out to be a man around fifty years old, with piercing black eyes and closely cropped dark hair, neatly hidden under a black hat. His formal black suit and calm, confident posture emphasized a hidden strength of character. His face—stern and impenetrable—showed the expression of a man accustomed to keeping situations under control.

Edgar invited Maxwell into the study. Once they were both seated, Maxwell removed his hat and, looking Edgar in the eye, began to speak:

"I understand that finding those documents raises questions," he began calmly. "I assure you that all of my agreements with Richard were strictly business-related and always honest."

Edgar watched his face closely, trying to catch any hidden motives.

"We're interested in what your role was in his business and why you've returned now, after his passing," Edgar asked directly.

Maxwell tilted his head slightly, his tone remaining steady.

"It's simple," he replied. "At one time, I was his partner and supported him through the most challenging moments. Yes, we had terms and commitments, which Richard fulfilled honorably to the end. But with his passing, unresolved questions remain, and I needed to clarify where things stand with his heirs."

Martin, who was present at the conversation, spoke with a slight tension in his voice.

"So, you're saying you have no intention of making claims or demanding anything from the family?"

Maxwell looked at him and replied calmly:

"I'm here simply to remind them of the agreements we made. If the family needs my assistance or explanations, I'm open to discussion. I have no intention of demanding anything that isn't rightfully mine."

Edgar studied Maxwell, seeming to catch a hint of regret in him.

"So, your return is merely a formality?" he asked.

Maxwell nodded.

"Exactly. I need nothing more than adherence to the agreements, and I don't intend to interfere with their affairs. All I ask is to finish what was started."

This conversation brought a sense of calm to the house: Maxwell's assured and reserved tone created the impression that he was not a threat, but simply fulfilling a duty to Richard's memory.

After the meeting with Maxwell and the initial conversation with Martin, Edgar sensed that there was far more hidden in the Lancaster family story than a mere business agreement. It was as though deep cracks lay beneath the calm surface of the family legacy.

Edgar paused, considering his next question, and unexpectedly asked:

"Martin, do you know of any threats that Richard might have received before his death? Was there anything that would've forced him to take drastic measures?"

Martin sighed, lowering his eyes.

"A couple of weeks before his death, Richard came to me. He looked worried, as if something was going on behind his back. It turned out he had received an anonymous warning—a letter saying that if he didn't take certain steps, his family would be in danger."

Edgar listened carefully to his words.

"And how did he respond?"

"At first, he wanted to handle it on his own," Martin replied, "but he soon admitted he had no idea where to start. It seemed like someone from his past intended to ruin everything he'd built. I suggested he speak with Maxwell, but he refused, believing that Maxwell wasn't the only threat."

These words set Edgar on edge. If Richard suspected someone else, then he likely viewed the threat as more than just financial.

Edgar paused to think, then asked:

"And are you certain that Richard didn't confide in anyone about these threats?"

Martin hesitated before answering:

"He only mentioned one person. The last time we spoke about it, Richard said, 'There's someone in the family who's willing to do anything to take my legacy.'"

These words hung in the silence as Edgar processed what he'd heard. It seemed that not only were there internal conflicts brewing in the house, but someone might be using Maxwell's return as a chance to remove competitors.

Suddenly, a knock on the door interrupted them, and Lucy Lancaster entered, looking anxious. She shot a quick glance at Martin and Edgar.

"Sorry to interrupt, but I noticed that someone had gone into my father's study again. One of the documents left on the desk is missing," her voice trembled, and she quickly turned away to hide her distress.

Edgar and Martin exchanged wary glances. It was clear that someone in the house had started to act—perhaps even to cover their tracks before the truth could come to light.

Later that evening, as Edgar and Martin discussed the missing document, Edgar noticed a thin folder wedged between the pages of a large book left at the edge of Richard's desk. He opened it, expecting to see another financial report, but after glancing at the first few pages, he froze.

The document was dated over twenty years ago, and it bore a name he didn't recognize. It was an official acknowledgment of paternity: Richard Lancaster confirmed that he was the father of a child named Thomas Grayson. Edgar read on, realizing that Richard had pledged to support his son financially, but had never brought him into the family.

Edgar quickly closed the folder and turned to Martin, who was watching his reaction with interest.

"Martin, how long have you known about this?" he asked, barely concealing the tension in his voice.

Martin sighed and looked away.

"Richard asked me not to speak of it, but… yes, I knew. Thomas is his son, but due to complicated relations with his mother, Richard decided to keep it secret. As far as I know, he only provided for him financially. But Thomas himself may not even know who his father was."

Edgar understood that the emergence of Thomas could seriously jeopardize the standing of the other family members, who had always considered themselves the sole heirs.

"And now," Edgar said quietly, "with Richard gone, his past has begun to shape this family's future."

After the unexpected discovery in Richard's study, Edgar had no doubt that Thomas Grayson's appearance could seriously jeopardize the standing of the other family members, who had always considered themselves the sole heirs. Now that Richard was gone, his past was beginning to shape the future of everyone in the mansion. Trying to sort things out, Edgar decided to conduct a few conversations to better understand the situation.

He first invited Evelyn—he needed confirmation for his assumption that Thomas was a child born during their marriage. When Evelyn entered, her evident wariness was understandable.

"Evelyn," he began carefully, "I need to discuss something concerning your husband. Tell me, were you aware of any connections Richard might have had outside of the family? During the time you were already married?"

She froze, her face paling.

"What exactly are you asking, Edgar?"

Edgar took out the folder, without revealing its contents, and quietly replied:

"I found documents confirming Richard's paternity to someone named Thomas Grayson. According to these documents, Richard acknowledged him as his son 25 years ago. Did you know about this?"

Evelyn didn't respond right away. She turned away, her face contorted with suppressed anger.

"Yes," she finally muttered through clenched teeth. "I knew. He was... weak for her. Richard said it was a mistake, but when that boy was born, he took responsibility. He promised me he'd never allow it to disrupt our peace. But now, it seems he didn't keep even that promise."

Edgar understood that this was a painful, contentious subject for her. He gave her a moment to collect herself, then continued:

"Thank you for your honesty, Evelyn. This is important. I see now that the situation is more complicated than I expected."

After Evelyn, Edgar decided to speak with Andrew to find out if he knew of his half-brother's existence. When Andrew entered the study, his face showed a trace of irritation.

"I'd like to ask you, Andrew, if you're aware that your father may have had another heir?"

Andrew visibly tensed.

"Heir? Besides Lucy and me? What are you talking about?"

Edgar studied his reaction, then replied:

"This is about someone who, according to the documents, may be your half-brother."

Andrew leaned back in his chair, his face reflecting a mix of anger and shock.

"So you're telling me that someone else could claim a share of the inheritance? How... how is that even possible?"

Edgar understood that Andrew's reaction to the appearance of a half-brother was more than just a surprise—it was a real threat to him. The possibility of another heir could change everything Andrew had come to think of as his own. To sort out the situation and confirm the existence of Thomas Grayson, Edgar decided to find this person and discover if he even knew his true origins.

Chapter 6: Illegitimate Legacy

The next day, Edgar found Thomas Grayson's address among Richard's old records. He lived in a small town nearby, and Edgar decided to go there immediately. Upon arriving, Edgar found himself at a neat house with a well-kept garden, clearly tended to with care by its owner.

When the door opened, a young man about twenty-five years old stood before Edgar, with dark eyes and a calm yet wary expression. In his features, Edgar immediately noticed a resemblance to Richard's photos—the same focused gaze and restrained strength in every movement.

"Hello, Thomas?" Edgar began cautiously.

Thomas nodded slightly, clearly surprised by the unfamiliar guest.

"Yes, that's me. How can I help?"

Edgar decided to get straight to the point, not dragging out the conversation.

"My name is Edgar Drake. I'm investigating recent events concerning the Richard Lancaster family. And according to documents, I learned that Richard... he was your father."

Thomas's face froze for a moment. He closed the door behind Edgar, then slowly sank into a chair, as if trying to process what he'd just heard.

"I... I knew my father was someone important, but we never met," he said quietly, avoiding Edgar's gaze. "My mother told me he wanted to stay distant, but he cared for me from afar. I always assumed he didn't care."

Drake listened attentively, analyzing each word.

"How do you feel about the fact that now, after his death, you have a right to a share of the inheritance?" he asked.

Thomas chuckled bitterly.

"Inheritance? I never thought about it. I grew up knowing I didn't have a family and learned to rely on myself. What would an inheritance mean from a man I never knew?"

Drake saw in Thomas an absence of greed, but also a strength of character that could seriously change the situation for everyone involved.

Edgar studied Thomas closely, realizing that this young man could become a pivotal figure, one most of the family members had never even suspected. Thomas seemed lost in thought, processing the news that his father had been part of the powerful Lancaster family.

Drake continued the conversation, careful not to pressure Thomas.

"Thomas, do you think that if you'd known who your father was, you would have wanted to meet him? Or perhaps claim any rights?"

Thomas paused, then shook his head.

"No, I'm not looking for any rights or inheritance. I wasn't part of that family, and I don't need it. I've always lived independently and don't want to get involved in their affairs. It's... someone else's story, not mine."

Edgar nodded, assessing his sincerity. Thomas truly didn't seem like someone interested in family intrigue. But his very existence could still change everything.

"I understand, Thomas. However, there's a chance that someone from the family might seek you out. Knowing your origins, you could become more than just an outsider—you might be a threat to those currently vying for Richard's legacy."

Thomas visibly tensed, feeling the weight of his words.

"You mean someone in the family... might want to get rid of me?"

Edgar responded calmly:

"I don't know yet. But in the Lancaster family, there are those for whom you represent a threat."

These words gave Thomas pause. Now Edgar Drake saw that the young man would have to make a difficult choice: either stay on the sidelines or investigate the legacy he unexpectedly found himself tied to.

After meeting Thomas, Edgar decided to find his mother to understand what kind of mark Richard had left on their lives. He hoped she could reveal who else might have known about Thomas and why Richard had chosen secrecy.

Thomas's mother, Mary Grayson, lived on the outskirts of the same town. Her home was simple and cozy—a modest setting that showed the years of patient work within its walls. Mary greeted Edgar cautiously but agreed to talk when he introduced himself and explained his purpose.

When they were both seated at a small table in her living room, Mary sighed and, looking at Edgar, began:

"I knew this day would come eventually. Richard always lived a double life—one for the world and another for us. He promised to take care of Thomas, but he warned he wouldn't be able to bring him into his family."

Edgar nodded, listening intently.

"Why did he make that choice? Was there something holding him back?"

Mary smiled bitterly.

"He was afraid of losing his reputation. Richard loved us, but his family and his position were more important. He said that one day Thomas would be able to make himself known, but only on one condition: that his children would never learn about him."

Edgar sensed the tension in her words and asked gently:

"Do you think someone in his family would see Thomas as a threat?"

Mary hesitated for a moment, then her face turned serious.

"I think so. Richard told me that in his family, money and power meant too much. He feared Thomas might be in danger if anyone ever found out about him. Maybe he was right."

Edgar listened carefully, realizing that Mary was worried for her son. Now he understood that Richard had tried to protect Thomas from family intrigue, but that secrecy might have turned into a new threat after Richard was gone.

Drake left Mary Grayson's house, understanding that he now had a new detail in his possession, one that could turn the investigation in an unexpected direction. Returning to the mansion, he noticed that the atmosphere among the family members was growing increasingly tense. Their suspicious and wary looks revealed that recent events had made each of them consider who might actually pose a threat.

That evening, Edgar Drake gathered everyone in the library. Evelyn, Andrew, Lucy, Oliver, Amelia and Martin Hudson took their seats, each in their own chair, and all eyes were fixed on Edgar as he prepared to ask questions that could reveal their true motives.

Edgar began calmly, yet firmly:

"I have learned things about Richard's past, actions that could have consequences for all of you. I'm talking about a person who is also his heir. This person may not be seeking inheritance, but his very existence has already changed your family's situation."

Evelyn cast a quick glance at Andrew before turning back to Edgar.

"I assumed everything was settled," she said, her voice tense. "We knew nothing about this… person, and I doubt he has any right to what belongs to us."

Andrew crossed his arms over his chest, his face grim.

"If he shows up here, what will it change for us? He wasn't part of our family. And if he thinks he can just come in and stake a claim…"

Drake interrupted, trying to keep the situation under control.

"I'm not certain he's interested in the inheritance. However, it seems that someone here may have known about him earlier and could be pursuing their own goals."

Silence hung in the room as Edgar observed their reactions. He waited as the silence in the room grew heavier. He could tell that the news had shocked everyone present, but one of them was hiding their true intentions better than the others.

Finally, Lucy broke the silence, her voice trembling:

"What do you mean by that, Mr. Drake? Are you saying someone here knew about this beforehand? But how… how is that possible?"

Edgar looked at her intently.

"Some of your surprise seems genuine," he said. "But it's not just about who learned of Thomas's existence first; it's about someone potentially using this hidden knowledge to their advantage."

Martin, who had been silently observing until then, finally spoke up:

"If we are indeed talking about an heir who was never part of the family, he's unlikely to want to fight for the inheritance. But if someone has used this against us…"

Evelyn gave a stifled sigh, and Andrew cast a quick look at her, one in which Edgar caught a trace of doubt.

"Mother, did you know about this?" he asked, his voice sharper than usual.

Evelyn looked at her son, trying to hide her irritation.

"No, Andrew, I knew nothing," she replied coolly. "And if anyone here is hiding the truth, it's certainly not me."

Drake understood that the conversation was on the brink of revealing deeper conflicts. He needed to steer it in the right direction to expose any weak links.

"If the truth comes out," he said, looking at each of them, "everyone will have to accept the changes it brings."

Oliver, seated at the corner of the table, suddenly reached into his pocket and pulled out a small medallion wrapped in an old cloth. His face was focused, and, carefully unwrapping the cloth, he slowly raised the medallion so everyone could see.

"I found this among grandfather's old things," Oliver said. "The initials 'T. G.' are engraved on the back. I didn't know anything about it until I stumbled across it in his study. No one ever told me about it."

Edgar leaned in for a closer look at the item and noticed the antique, faded gold finish on the medallion. This item was clearly significant and, perhaps, belonged to Thomas or his mother—a symbol of a hidden connection to the Lancaster family.

Evelyn looked at the medallion, and her face turned pale. Her hands trembled, as if this medallion awakened memories she had tried to forget.

"Where exactly did you find this?" her voice broke, and she quickly turned away, hiding her agitation.

Oliver gave her a searching look.

"Among grandfather's papers. It was tucked away in the farthest corner, as if it was meant to stay hidden from everyone."

Lucy looked at her mother with concern and asked:

"Mother, do you know who this medallion belonged to?"

Evelyn nervously averted her gaze, her hands trembling slightly. It seemed she was struggling with herself not to answer right away. The rest of the family waited tensely for her reaction.

Finally, gathering her thoughts, Evelyn spoke in a quiet but firm voice:

"This medallion once belonged to Thomas's mother… Richard gave it to her as a symbol of their connection, but I didn't know it still existed. I thought it had disappeared when she left our lives."

Drake noticed her words stirred a wave of unease among the others. He decided to use the moment to ask:

"Evelyn, have you ever seen what's inside the medallion? Perhaps there's information Richard wanted to keep hidden."

Evelyn nodded, struggling to look at Edgar.

"Yes, I've seen it. On the inside of the medallion…" her voice faltered for a moment, "there's an engraved code. I don't know what it leads to, but Richard always said it was the key to 'forgiving' his mistakes."

Andrew frowned, interrupting her:

"Enough with the riddles, Mother. If there's something he wanted to keep, we need to find out."

Edgar realized that the code on the medallion might point to a hidden compartment where Richard could have concealed his will or other important documents. He announced this to those present and suggested that everyone move to Richard's study to search for the safe.

When they all entered the study, Drake carefully examined the room, knowing Richard wouldn't have left such crucial documents in plain sight. His gaze traveled over every detail of the room: the bookshelves filled with books, the massive desk where Richard worked, the paintings on the walls.

He began by methodically inspecting each painting, one by one, hoping to find a hidden mechanism that might reveal a secret compartment. But behind the paintings was only an ordinary wall. Then, he systematically checked each shelf on the bookcase, pulling out books and examining their backs, hoping to find a hidden slot. It was all in vain.

When Drake returned to Richard's massive desk, he opened each drawer, pulling them all the way out, but there were only documents and old letters. Finally, he got down on his knees and felt along the floor under the desk. His hand came across a small indentation in the wood, almost invisible to the naked eye.

He carefully pressed it, and with a barely audible click, a section of the floor lifted, revealing a small compartment. It had a digital lock requiring a code. Edgar took out the medallion, checked the engraved code, and entered the numbers. A second later, the lock clicked, and he lifted the lid.

Drake took a thin leather folder from the compartment and opened it cautiously. Among the papers was a will clearly naming Thomas as an official heir, equal to the other family members. But the assembled group froze when they saw another name—Mary

Grayson, to whom Richard had left a significant portion of his assets and funds.

Andrew shook his head indignantly.

"So he knew he was going? Why didn't he tell us anything?"

Edgar looked at Andrew, keeping his composure.

"Perhaps he didn't have time. His death was premature, and likely unexpected."

Chapter 7: The Will and Its Consequences

After the revelation of the will, the atmosphere in the study grew more tense. Edgar carefully observed each person's reaction, trying to understand who among them seemed most disturbed by the new distribution of the inheritance.

Andrew was the first to break the silence:

"So, all this time, Father was hiding the fact that he had another son? And on top of that, a significant portion of the inheritance goes to Mary?" His voice trembled with resentment.

Lucy shook her head nervously.

"This can't be... Why did he keep us in the dark?" She turned to Evelyn, who stood slightly hunched to the side, as if deep in thought.

Evelyn looked tensely at Edgar and asked:

"Is it possible that this will is a forgery? Richard would have warned us if he intended to leave everything to this boy and his mother!"

Edgar considered this for a moment, then replied:

"The will appears genuine, and the code in the medallion confirms that Richard hid it himself. But what interests me is something else: who knew about this will before we discovered it? Perhaps he truly intended to tell you, but someone intervened."

This thought hung in the air, like a heavy cloud, and Edgar felt that the situation was becoming increasingly dangerous.

As silence settled over the room, Edgar noticed Evelyn cross her arms over her chest. Her face remained expressionless, but her eyes showed tension. She stepped forward, drawing attention to herself once more.

"If the will is indeed genuine," she said evenly, "then Richard intended not only to keep these changes hidden, but to protect them from us in some way."

Lucy continued looking at her mother, her face filled with worry.

"But why would he do that? What's so special about this will that he couldn't bring himself to discuss it with us?"

Edgar took a deep breath, trying to piece it all together.

"I suspect that Richard meant to keep this will hidden until it truly became necessary. If someone discovered it prematurely… that might have provided motive."

Andrew frowned, glancing suspiciously at everyone present.

"So you're saying that one of us already knew?"

Evelyn stepped forward and took a deep breath.

"Yes," she said quietly, "I knew about the will. Richard entrusted me with this secret, but I swear, I had nothing to do with his death."

Those present exchanged suspicious glances, and a shadow of doubt touched everyone. Andrew and Lucy shared worried looks, while Miller watched Evelyn's reaction closely.

After a brief pause, Evelyn added:

"If this is what Richard wanted, then I believe we should accept this will."

The room was filled with tense silence. Edgar looked around at everyone present, noting how each of them tried to hide their own thoughts.

Andrew looked at his mother with disbelief.

"Are you sure this is really what he wanted? To leave us without warning, with such... a secret decision?"

Evelyn held his gaze calmly.

"Yes, exactly that, Andrew."

Lucy turned to Edgar.

"But what if this will is indeed a forgery? How can we be sure?"

Edgar stepped closer to the table, holding the will in his hands.

"The authenticity of the document can be verified. But I'll say it again: the code in the medallion was correct, and this indicates that Richard hid it himself."

Andrew clenched his fists, barely containing his frustration.

"So now we're just supposed to accept this? Accept that Father was ready to leave half of his fortune to people we don't even know?"

Evelyn sighed, her gaze remaining steady.

"We have no right to dispute his will. And don't forget, we're talking about your half-brother, no matter how much you may want to deny his existence."

Lucy spoke quietly.

"But why didn't he ever tell us? Is this really fair?"

Edgar stepped forward, sensing that the tension in the room was building with each passing second.

"It's not a matter of fairness, but of why Richard decided to do this. He kept this will hidden—perhaps he was waiting for the right moment. Or perhaps someone found out about it early and decided to take advantage."

Miller added, looking at Andrew and Lucy:

"The will isn't finalized immediately, and we still have a chance to uncover the truth."

Miller's words hung in the silence, and Edgar noticed how the faces of those present reflected a mixture of tension and suspicion. He knew that each of them might now wonder if someone had decided to get rid of Richard upon discovering this hidden will.

Andrew was the first to break:

"If someone was willing to kill for this inheritance, then none of us can feel safe here."

Edgar looked at him closely.

"Perhaps that's why Richard chose to keep the will hidden, to leave it only in the event of his sudden death. He knew the truth could tear the family apart, but he might have hoped that by revealing it himself, he could soften the consequences."

Evelyn frowned, her voice firm.

"We must follow his final wishes. If he chose this will, he must have had his reasons."

Lucy nodded, but her gaze remained cautious, and she quietly added:

"If he had good reasons, then we need to find out what they were."

Edgar sensed the tension in the room reaching its peak. He took a breath and slowly looked at each person present.

"The will remains a crucial piece of evidence," he finally said. "But beyond the will, there may be something else connecting recent events to Richard's past. We still don't know what he was hiding, or what else might be in his documents."

Miller nodded and suggested:

"Perhaps we should examine other personal papers of Richard's, those not included in the will. They might contain information shedding light on his decisions."

Evelyn flinched slightly but quickly composed herself.

"If it helps reveal the truth, then review whatever's needed. Just don't let it destroy this family completely."

Andrew stood up, looking determinedly at Edgar.

"I won't allow a secretly drafted will to create even more conflict. If necessary, I'll help with the search."

After a brief discussion, Edgar, Miller, and Andrew decided to continue examining Richard's personal documents in his study. They focused on a small cabinet next to his desk, where, according to Andrew, Richard kept his most important papers.

Edgar took the first folder from the top shelf and opened it. At first glance, it contained regular reports, company documents, and previous versions of wills. However, at the end of the folder, he found an envelope marked: "Private. For family only."

Judging by the silence, all three realized that the answers to their questions might lie inside. Edgar slowly opened the envelope and found a letter written in Richard's handwriting. The text was brief but meaningful.

"If you're reading this letter, it means I'm gone. My decisions may shock you, but know that I acted in the family's best interests. No one should try to change my will, and if circumstances have turned otherwise, know—this is no coincidence.

There were people in my life whom I should have acknowledged. Now, it is your task to accept the truth."

Andrew clenched his teeth, processing what he'd read.

"Wow..," he said quietly, trying to contain his anger. "But why did he stay silent?"

Edgar looked at Andrew carefully and replied:

"It seems he feared his revelations might tear the family apart, and he hoped that time would ease the pain."

Miller nodded:

"So, Richard was trying to control even what would happen after his death."

After finding the letter, Edgar, Andrew, and Miller stood in silence, processing the facts that had come to light. Andrew turned suspiciously to Martin, who had been observing everything in silence, and then to Amelia.

"Martin, as Father's lawyer, did you know about this hidden will? How is it that we're only hearing about it now?" Andrew struggled to hide his irritation.

Martin sighed, stepping back slightly.

"Yes, I helped Richard draft it. He felt it needed to remain secret, at least until the right time came. Both Amelia and I were aware, but we were bound to keep it confidential. Only Richard could decide when and how to reveal its contents."

Evelyn narrowed her eyes, her voice laced with slight suspicion.

"So, you knew Richard had other heirs? And you kept this from the family?"

Amelia, standing aside, lowered her gaze.

"We had no other choice. As his personal assistant, I knew some details but not everything. When he changed the will, he warned me that the consequences could be severe. But... I had no idea it would lead to this."

Edgar nodded, noting each person's reaction. Martin and Amelia's words only confirmed how deliberate Richard's decision had been and how carefully he had kept it hidden.

At that moment, the door opened quietly, and Geraldine entered the study. She glanced at everyone in the room, noticing the documents in Edgar's hands, and asked calmly:

"Looks like I missed something important?"

Edgar looked up, raising an eyebrow slightly.

"You returned so quickly, Geraldine. It seems your secret trip concerning Simon's affairs didn't take much time?"

Geraldine nodded, her expression serious.

"I found some information that might clarify his financial matters and point to people with whom he had unfinished dealings. But it seems that new questions have arisen here as well?"

Geraldine moved to the center of the room, feeling the tense gazes of those gathered. She held a brief pause, then, without wasting any time, began her account.

"While I was handling Simon's affairs, I managed to uncover some very intriguing documents," she began, her voice quiet but confident. "It turns out that shortly before his death, Simon entered into a contract with a private investor. Interestingly, this person is linked to financial schemes that have caused significant losses to the family in recent years."

Edgar listened closely, each new fact arousing even more suspicion in him.

"Who is this investor?" he asked, barely containing his interest.

Geraldine met his gaze, then slowly answered:

"Maxwell Hunt."

A tense silence hung over the room. Maxwell had already revealed himself to be a mysterious figure, but now his involvement in Simon's finances raised even more questions.

"So Simon knew about the schemes and perhaps even threatened to expose him?" Miller suggested.

Geraldine nodded.

"Judging by the documents, Simon was conducting his own investigation. He likely hoped to use the information he gathered to protect his own interests."

Edgar cast a careful glance at Martin and Amelia, watching their reaction to Maxwell Hunt's involvement. It seemed this was news to everyone.

Andrew asked reservedly, "So, Simon decided to act on his own? And he knew that Maxwell could be a danger to the family?"

Geraldine nodded, choosing her words.

"Yes, but it seems he underestimated the scope of the threat. Judging by the information he gathered, Simon planned to use it as leverage, but the closer he got to the truth, the more dangerous it became."

Edgar pondered, piecing the facts together.

"So, Simon walked into a trap, trying to protect the family. Perhaps he counted on someone in the house to help him?" Edgar looked at Geraldine questioningly.

She paused before responding calmly, "For now, it's just my assumption, but Simon knew he was taking a risk. His documents could explain a lot."

After the conversation, everyone returned to their rooms. Drake and Miller remained in the study, discussing the facts that had come to light and trying to piece everything together. In the silence of the night, they both felt that with each new discovery, the hidden secrets grew ever more dangerous.

Not half an hour had passed when a piercing scream echoed through the house. Drake and Miller rushed toward the sound. Arriving in the hallway, they found Geraldine in her room—she was in shock, barely able to stand, her face pale.

"Someone tried to attack me," she said, her voice shaking but trying to remain steady. "I came out of the bathroom, and… in the glow of the floor lamp, I saw a figure holding a knife. I screamed, and the person immediately jumped out the window."

Edgar noticed how the curtains swayed in the night breeze. Approaching the window, he checked—it was wide open, as if someone had hurriedly exited the room.

After this incident, a strict curfew was imposed in the house. With nightfall, all occupants were strictly forbidden from leaving their rooms after dinner, and windows were to be kept closed. Drake and Miller announced that they would make rounds at 11:00 p.m. to check on each room and ensure everyone's safety.

Later, reflecting on what had happened, Edgar sensed that Geraldine had clearly left something unsaid.

Chapter 8: Edges of Truth

The next morning, a heavy silence hung over the house. Drake and Miller decided to act quickly to prevent fear from overtaking the occupants. They walked through the house, checking the windows and doors, discussing the details of the attempt on Geraldine.

Edgar stopped at her door and knocked. Geraldine looked tired but determined.

"We understand that the threat is real, Geraldine. If you remember any details about the person you saw, please tell us now," Edgar said.

She nodded, hesitating.

"I didn't see the face, but... there was something about his posture. Very familiar, as if I'd seen him before." Geraldine started, as if recalling something important. "I think I could recognize him if I saw him again."

Miller and Edgar exchanged glances.

"Anything else you haven't told us?" Edgar asked, his interest rising.

Geraldine paused and quietly added:

"The thing is, Simon had hidden papers. They concerned Richard and... a person possibly connected to asset schemes."

Edgar looked closely at Geraldine, as if trying to read her thoughts.

"Where exactly did Simon keep these papers?" he asked.

Geraldine thought for a moment, frowning.

"He mentioned hiding them where no one would think to look. Perhaps in one of the old rooms where his personal belongings are kept. I believe they could be in his study or even in the basement."

Edgar nodded, considering her words.

"All right. Miller and I will begin the search. These papers may shed light on the events that led to his death."

Geraldine hesitated before adding:

"Just be careful. Simon left me a hint that someone was watching him."

Drake and Miller, having checked the upper floors, decided that Simon's papers might be hidden in the basement. The way there led through a narrow hallway, exuding dampness and staleness—like the space itself had long since absorbed all the house's secrets.

Miller held the flashlight, illuminating the area around them, while Edgar walked ahead, scrutinizing every corner. He stopped, noticing rows of shelves covered in a thick layer of dust.

"Something tells me Simon wasn't the type to trust everyone with his secrets," Edgar murmured, examining the shelves. "No one's been down here for a long time."

Miller nodded, pointing the flashlight at an old shelf filled with boxes and worn folders.

"If I were hiding something, I'd definitely choose the farthest corner," he said with a smile. "Maybe Simon thought the same way?"

Edgar smirked.

"You're right—people like him often follow one rule: the farther, the safer."

He carefully pulled on one of the boxes when a creak suddenly echoed, and the shelf began to sway dangerously. Before he could pull his hand back, pieces of wood and dust began to rain down from above. Drake and Miller barely managed to jump back.

Miller, brushing himself off, muttered grimly,

"Quite a coincidence. Or maybe someone left us a little 'gift'?"

Drake looked over the shelf, his gaze falling on a small bundle barely visible among the dust and debris. He reached out, carefully retrieving the bundle. The cloth it was wrapped in looked faded with age and had a musty smell. He unfolded it, revealing a small stack of papers tied with a black ribbon.

Miller, leaning in close, whistled.

"Looks like we found his records. Now we just need to figure out what Simon was hiding so carefully."

Edgar nodded, quickly flipping through the papers. The pages were filled with small notes and symbols that seemed random. But one detail caught his attention: Maxwell Hunt's name appeared in one of the documents, along with a sequence of numbers that resembled a cipher.

"Take a look," Edgar showed Miller the page. "I think this code was used for some critical deal or to access important information. It may have been Simon's plan."

Miller frowned.

"So, Simon was planning to deal with Maxwell on his own?"

Drake and Miller, carefully studying the papers, noticed that among the numerous notes, one code was highlighted as if it held special significance. Edgar pondered.

"We need to check if this cipher opens access to some kind of archive or even a bank account of Simon's. If he really intended to use it against Maxwell, then this is likely the key to the entire story."

Miller nodded.

"But if Maxwell or someone in the family knows about this code, they'll surely try to interfere."

They decided to return to the office and check the code found among Simon's papers. Edgar connected the laptop to the power supply and entered the code from the bundle. Finally, the screen opened to reveal Simon's archive, filled with files and documents. Drake and Miller looked intently at the list: it was full of business notes and financial records.

"There it is... it looks like we've found his personal archive," Miller whispered, exchanging glances with Edgar.

They began browsing the files, and after a few minutes, Edgar came across a folder marked "Deal with Hunt".

Edgar opened the folder marked "Deal with Hunt," and a series of emails, contracts, and financial documents dated nearly a decade ago appeared on the screen. Inside were numerous attachments, some copies of contracts and others personal correspondence between Simon and Maxwell Hunt.

Miller leaned in, examining the lines of text.

"It doesn't look like they were just business partners," he noted quietly. "Look, there are mentions of payments that clearly go beyond regular agreements."

Edgar read several emails in which Hunt demanded that Simon urgently transfer funds if he didn't want certain information to become public. In one of the last messages, Simon replied curtly and with an edge of threat:

"If you go against me, you'll be risking far more than I will."

Miller raised his eyebrows in surprise.

"So they were blackmailing each other."

Edgar closed the email and continued browsing the folder, hoping to find more information that might explain what Maxwell was blackmailing Simon with. His attention was drawn to records of secret financial transfers to an account registered under the initials "M.G."

"Look at this, Miller. This could be a lead," Edgar murmured. "The sums are substantial, and the transfers were made regularly."

Miller looked at the screen, puzzled.

"So not only was Simon connected to Hunt, but he was also funding someone with these initials. And from the look of these transfers, it's been going on for a long time."

Edgar nodded, scrolling through the other files. Finally, he came across an encrypted folder labeled "Project Grayson."

Edgar tried to open the encrypted folder labeled "Project Grayson," but the system requested an additional password. He paused, trying to make sense of what he was seeing. The name Grayson had already come up before—it was tied to the paternity claim for Thomas, Richard's secret son. This folder might hold answers that could shed light on even deeper family secrets.

Miller, noticing Edgar's hesitation, said:

"You think this is connected to the inheritance? Maybe Simon found information that could jeopardize other heirs?"

Edgar nodded.

"Seems that way. We have the medallion code, and it might be linked to access here."

He entered the code, and a moment later, the "Project Grayson" folder opened.

Opening the "Project Grayson" folder, Drake and Miller found several files marked with different dates. Inside were document scans, records of fund transfers, and a few audio files. One file titled "Heir Rights" caught Edgar's particular attention.

He opened it and saw a contract stating that Thomas Grayson was an acknowledged heir of Richard Lancaster. The agreement confirmed a commitment to financially support Thomas and outlined his rights to a share of the family's assets.

Miller leaned closer to the screen and read aloud:

"'By this agreement, Thomas is granted the right to the Lancaster inheritance, regardless of the will of other family members.'"

Edgar examined the text closely.

"It seems Simon knew the will had been altered in Thomas's favor."

Edgar scrolled through the files and came across a video labeled "Confidential." He exchanged a glance with Miller, took a breath, and hit play.

On the screen appeared Simon sitting at his desk in that very office. Judging by the setting, it was recorded by a hidden camera, and soon Maxwell Hunt came into view. They sat facing each other, and even on the recording, the tension was palpable.

Simon's voice was sharp:

"Maxwell, I'm done playing by your rules. If you keep threatening me, I'll tell the family that you've been deceiving them all this time."

Maxwell looked calm, but his tone was laced with warning:

"You don't understand what you're toying with, Simon. Your threats will turn against you. If anyone finds out about this too soon, the consequences will be disastrous not just for you."

Drake and Miller watched intently, trying to capture every detail of this tense dialogue.

Simon didn't waver under Maxwell's pressure. He leaned closer, determination etched on his face:

"You've underestimated me, Maxwell. I have proof of your schemes, and I won't stay silent. If you don't back down, I'll bring everything to light—for the family, and the police."

A hint of irritation flickered across Maxwell's face, but he quickly collected himself, smirked, and leaned back in his chair:

"If you choose to go against me, Simon, you'll have to sacrifice a lot. Do you really think the family will be pleased to know the truth about you? We have more in common than you think."

Edgar paused the video, processing what he'd just seen.

"So Maxwell wasn't just blackmailing him—they held each other in a trap," Miller noted thoughtfully. "If someone found out about their plan, that could be a motive for murder."

Edgar nodded and resumed the video, hoping to hear something even more revealing.

"Remember, Simon," Maxwell said, "if anyone finds out about this will too soon, Thomas will suffer first. Make sure you're ready for the consequences."

The video ended, leaving Drake and Miller in thoughtful silence.

They stared at the blank screen, digesting what they'd just heard. Maxwell's words about Thomas being the first victim sounded especially ominous. Simon had clearly understood the risks and had tried to protect Thomas, but now it was evident that their hidden agreements had turned into a deadly trap for all involved.

Miller broke the silence first:

"So, Simon decided to stand his ground, but maybe he didn't have a chance to tell anyone what he was planning."

Edgar nodded, still focused on the screen.

"And it seems Maxwell was ready to go to any lengths to protect his secrets. If someone else knew about this meeting, they'd have a motive to silence them both."

Edgar checked the remaining video files and soon found another one—a much shorter file marked "Backup Plan." He tried to play it again, but it wouldn't load—a message popped up indicating that the file was damaged or partially deleted. He closed the video with a frustrated sigh.

"It seems the most crucial evidence has been lost."

Miller shook his head grimly:

"Looks like someone took care to keep things hidden. But this only proves that Simon was really trying to share information that could have turned things against Maxwell."

Edgar paused in thought, then suddenly stood up.

"We need to talk to Maxwell Hunt again. If he was willing to go to such lengths to keep the truth hidden, he might have had an accomplice among those in the house now."

Miller nodded.

"You think he managed to recruit someone in the family to keep his secrets?"

Edgar squinted, considering the situation.

"If Maxwell was indeed trying to maintain his influence, he could have had an accomplice. And if that person is a family member, they would have a double motive—to protect themselves and to continue benefiting from the inheritance."

Miller stroked his chin, thoughtfully staring at the folder of documents on the screen.

"In that case... maybe we should check Simon's call history and recent meetings. Some of them might have crossed paths with Maxwell frequently."

Edgar nodded in agreement.

"I think we should also look into which family members might have stayed under the radar but were influencing Simon and trying to steer events in their favor."

Drake and Miller decided to return to examining Simon's phone. After a few minutes of careful scrutiny, Edgar found an encrypted messaging app—a rare program usually used for secure, confidential conversations. Decoding the app wasn't easy, but soon they managed to access the message history.

The correspondence was with a contact identified only by the initial "M." The texts were short but menacing. The last message, sent to Simon the night before his death, read:

"You don't understand; this is not a game. Remember who controls the situation."

Miller squinted.

"It seems Simon really was in danger. And if 'M' is Maxwell, he clearly had a strong motive to silence Simon."

Edgar nodded, continuing to scroll through the messages. Some of them mentioned meetings at the house, hints about "old debts," and repeated threats.

Edgar carefully reviewed the exchanges, focusing on every word. Some of the texts were insistent, almost demanding immediate action:

"You've come too close to the edge. Decide, or we'll both lose everything."

The following messages were just as tense. Simon clearly didn't want to concede; his response read:

"I'm not backing down. Everyone will soon know what you're hiding."

Miller frowned.

"It seems they both understood that much more than money or property was at stake. And it was all tied to these 'old debts'… Do you think this connects to the will?"

Edgar nodded.

"Possibly, Simon was planning to expose Maxwell and anyone who was covering for him."

Edgar continued analyzing the messages, looking for anything that would shed light on Maxwell's motives. One message stood out from the rest of the threats:

"Don't forget, you're not the only one who stands to lose everything. Your family isn't ready for what I'll reveal."

Miller shook his head, clearly troubled.

"It seems Maxwell was blackmailing Simon not just over the inheritance. This is about something far more devastating for the whole family."

Edgar paused over this message, his gaze intense.

"It appears Maxwell knew secrets that could ruin the reputations of not just Simon but other family members. He might have been planning to use this as a final card to keep his influence."

Edgar took a deep breath, realizing that a confrontation with Maxwell might be the key to unraveling the whole scheme. He was now certain Maxwell was willing to use any means to maintain control over the Lancaster family's secrets. But one question remained: who in the family was helping him? For such a scheme, Maxwell would need someone who could stay out of sight yet was intimately aware of the family's affairs.

Miller interrupted his thoughts:

"So you think someone here was deliberately supporting Maxwell, helping him cover his tracks?"

Edgar nodded, considering their next steps.

— If there truly is an accomplice in this house, then they've likely been covering for Maxwell from the start, knowing his aims. Such a person is keen to protect not just their share but any information that could come out, Edgar replied.

Miller frowned, watching Edgar's reaction.

— So, our path is clear: we find the one who stands to lose the most if the family secrets come to light, he noted. — And it seems we need to carefully observe everyone here.

Edgar glanced at his watch.

— Perhaps we should begin with our evening rounds.

Drake and Miller began their evening rounds, slowly moving through the dark corridors of the mansion, illuminated only by dim wall lights. Each of the residents was already in their rooms; some looked sleepy, while others seemed alert, as though expecting something. Edgar paid close attention to every detail, searching for even the smallest hint of anything unusual.

As they reached Geraldine's room, Edgar sensed something odd — a faint but sharp chemical smell coming from her door. He held his breath for a moment and motioned for Miller.

— Do you smell that? he whispered.

Miller sniffed and nodded.

— Smells like a solvent or... something similar. Strange, given the setting. Maybe we should check if everything's alright with her?

They knocked, and a moment later, the door opened. Geraldine, still fully dressed, looked slightly surprised by their visit, but didn't seem to notice the smell.

— Is everything alright, Miss Lancaster? Edgar asked calmly, glancing around.

— Yes, of course. Has something happened? Geraldine replied.

Edgar noticed a faint white powdery line along the window frame, as though someone had recently tried to open it.

Edgar gave Miller a subtle nod toward the line on the window frame, and Miller responded with a slight nod, understanding exactly what had caught their attention. Edgar bent closer to the frame, carefully running his finger over the powder. He pondered for a moment and quietly said:

— Looks like someone recently tried to open the window. This powder... Maybe they left it intentionally to prevent the frame from creaking when opened or as a mark. This chemical smell could indicate someone attempted to pry open the window or left a sign, something noticeable upon inspection. The powder or substance might have been used to create a 'pathway' to Geraldine, but it seems something scared off the intruder, leaving their plan possibly incomplete.

Miller looked around carefully and shook his head grimly.

— So, someone might have tried to break in at night? Or maybe the mark was left for someone planning to leave?

Edgar looked back at Geraldine, standing expectantly, clearly unaware of anything.

— Did you notice anything unusual, Miss Lancaster? he asked cautiously, scanning her room, any strange sounds or smells?

Geraldine frowned, looking around.

— No, nothing like that. Although... lately, everything feels a bit unsettling, as if something's going on behind the scenes. But nothing specific, she answered, shaking her head.

Edgar surveyed the room once more, then calmly said:

— Please make sure to keep your windows closed at night, Miss Lancaster. Ensure they're locked. It's important.

Geraldine nodded, and Drake and Miller exited the room. Walking further down the hallway, Miller whispered:

"It looks like someone did indeed try to get in, but something might have stopped them. That powder… it was left in a hurry. Could it be someone from within the house?"

Edgar nodded, pondering who might have approached Geraldine's window and why they'd left that mark—a warning, or perhaps part of a more sinister plan?

Exchanging glances, Drake and Miller weighed their next steps.

"I think it would be logical to set up surveillance on her window tonight," Edgar said. "If someone tried to get to Geraldine's room, they might try again."

Miller nodded.

"I'll stay outside in the yard, and you keep an eye out from the hallway. If someone tries to come back, we'll be ready for them."

As night fell, the house plunged into silence. Edgar positioned himself at the end of the hallway, from where he had a clear view of the approach to Geraldine's room. Miller moved outside, concealing himself among the trees with a view of her window. Hours passed, the air growing colder, until the silence was finally broken by a faint rustling coming from the garden.

Miller tensed as he spotted a dim light from a flashlight cutting through the bushes. A figure in black crept toward Geraldine's window.

At that moment, Edgar, noticing movement outside, stood up and gave Miller their prearranged signal. The figure approached the window, and a quiet sound broke the stillness as they began to slide the frame open.

Miller advanced silently, without making a sound. Edgar, meanwhile, slipped through a side window to enter the room, positioning himself just a step away from the uninvited visitor.

The figure in black, already pushing open Geraldine's window, carefully reached inside, when Edgar suddenly turned on his flashlight, illuminating the intruder's face. It was Oliver, Andrew's son, who froze, clearly caught off guard.

"Oliver?" Edgar's voice was firm. "What are you doing here, in the middle of the night, by Geraldine's window?"

Oliver froze, his eyes darting between Drake and Miller, who was now approaching from the other side, blocking any escape. A few seconds of silence felt like an eternity.

"I... I just wanted to make sure she was all right," he mumbled, avoiding their gazes.

Drake and Miller exchanged wary looks.

"And you chose to do this by sneaking up at night?" Miller asked sarcastically. "You'd better tell us exactly what you're looking for here."

Oliver hesitated, realizing there was no way out of this.

Taking a deep breath, Oliver said quietly, looking away, "All right... the truth is, I was looking for something important. Not for myself... for the family."

Drake and Miller glanced at each other, intrigued, waiting for him to continue.

"Simon left something behind before he died," Oliver began. "Shortly before his death, he hinted that he had documents that could seriously change things for our family. They involve... business matters, debts. I've been trying to find them, but I couldn't access the study. I thought Geraldine might know something or have kept them here."

Edgar studied his reaction and finally spoke:

"If that's really what you were looking for, could it be so important that the family's safety might be at stake?"

Oliver nodded, struggling to keep his composure.

"I don't know the details, but it seemed to me he was trying to protect someone. He was tense and nervous. And before he disappeared, he said he would leave clues to help reveal the truth."

Miller gave a skeptical snort.

"So, you thought you'd search Geraldine's belongings at night to avoid being noticed?"

Oliver sighed and reluctantly nodded.

"Yes, I didn't want anyone in the family to see. To be honest, I'm afraid someone here might be connected to his death."

Edgar watched his every move closely.

"Why didn't you come to us right away? You knew you were taking a risk."

Oliver lowered his gaze and quietly said, "Because I still don't know who I can trust. Lately, everyone has been acting strangely, everyone hiding something. I think someone had been watching Simon for a long time… and now those eyes are on me."

Miller frowned, exchanging a glance with Edgar.

"So, you think you've become a target? Someone knows you're close to figuring this out?" Miller asked.

Oliver looked at them, clear anxiety in his eyes.

"Exactly. And if I can find the documents Simon left behind, I'll be able to discover who in our family is willing to do anything for the inheritance."

Эдгар and Miller listened intently as Oliver shared his suspicions and fears. The young man's words seemed to confirm their own suspicions—that the situation in the house might be even more dangerous than they had initially assumed.

Miller folded his arms, looking at Oliver with a hint of skepticism:

"So you're saying Simon left some documents behind? And you decided to search for them with Geraldine? Why did you think she might be involved?"

Oliver shook his head.

"I'm not sure… I just didn't know where else to look. Simon hardly left anything out in the open, but his last words—about 'signs' he would leave—kept bothering me. He was visibly anxious before he disappeared, and Geraldine always had access to the house and my grandfather's study. I thought he might have entrusted her with something or left it in her care."

Edgar pondered Oliver's words, realizing that every detail was crucial in the unfolding situation.

"You mentioned that Simon spoke about 'signs.' Do you have any idea what kind of signs he might have left?" Edgar asked.

Oliver hesitated, then answered carefully:

"He didn't say anything specific, but... he mentioned a 'key to the past.' He said that if anything happened to him, this 'key' would reveal who could be trusted."

Miller and Edgar exchanged glances, recognizing that the mystery might be more intricate than they had anticipated. It was possible that Simon had left clues that would not only reveal the motive but also help identify the person who posed a real threat.

Drake nodded, contemplating Oliver's words. In the "key to the past" that Simon had mentioned, the answers likely lay hidden. He sighed, turning to Miller.

"It seems all clues are leading us to his laptop. If there's information there about whom to trust, that's our next step."

Miller silently agreed, and they went to Simon's study to check the laptop.

Chapter 9: Unmasking

The detective and the officer entered the study. Drake nodded, contemplating Oliver's words. In the "key to the past" that Simon had mentioned, the answers likely lay hidden. He sighed, turning to Miller.

"It seems all clues are leading us to his laptop. If there's information there about whom to trust, that's our next step."

Miller silently agreed, and soon they found themselves back in the study before Simon's laptop. Edgar opened it, adjusted the settings to reveal hidden folders, and soon discovered five carefully concealed ones.

"'Medical Report,' 'Prenuptial Agreement,' 'Debt,' 'Finances,' and 'Bankruptcy,'" whispered Miller, nodding toward the screen. "It looks like he planned everything in detail."

Edgar clicked on the first folder, labeled "Medical Report." Inside, he found a file with a detailed report on Richard's health. Scanning the text, Edgar realized the data concealed crucial information: Richard's blood contained an unknown substance that had caused his death. The official medical report hadn't mentioned this, and it seemed Simon had hidden the report to prevent a scandal.

"That explains a lot," Miller whispered. "Someone orchestrated his death, and only Simon discovered the truth."

Closing the first folder, Edgar opened the next one, "Prenuptial Agreement." The document's text soon became clear: it was a contract between Mary and Maxwell Hunt. Under its terms, should she die, her entire estate would pass to Hunt, and her son Thomas was not included in the inheritance rights. Edgar clenched his fists, shocked at the blatant betrayal.

"So Hunt made a deal to secure his position from the start," murmured Miller. "Mary probably never knew how far he was willing to go."

Edgar silently closed the second folder and opened the third — "Debt." Inside, he found a file confirming that the Lancasters had completely repaid any debt to Maxwell. This discovery confirmed their suspicions: Hunt had been manipulating a nonexistent debt.

"Richard owed Hunt nothing. It was all a lie," remarked Edgar, shrugging. "Clearly, Simon intended to pass this information along to shatter Hunt's deception."

The next folder was "Finances." Edgar opened it and found a document showing that the Lancasters' finances were more than stable, with no outstanding debts. This implied that Hunt was spreading false rumors about the family's financial collapse.

"It looks like Hunt was banking on pressure and fear to keep the Lancasters under his control," concluded Miller.

Edgar nodded, moving on to the last folder—"Bankruptcy." Inside were reports showing Hunt's actual financial state: his business was on the brink of collapse, and he was entirely dependent on the Lancasters' money.

Edgar leaned back in his chair, taking a deep breath.

"So, this confirms Hunt's motives. He was controlling everything from the start, doing whatever he could to stay afloat."

Miller shook his head grimly, watching the screen.

"And most likely, he was willing to go to any lengths to keep access to the Lancasters' money. But that doesn't explain who in the house might have helped him if someone really knew about his plans."

Edgar gazed thoughtfully at the hidden documents.

"Hunt was cautious, but he obviously didn't expect us to reach this information. Based on what we found, he already knew his position was unstable. Now we just need to find out who he could have pulled into this scheme, promising benefits or persuading them it was for everyone's good."

Miller nodded, watching Edgar's reaction.

"I think it makes sense to speak to Oliver again. Maybe he overheard a conversation, or Hunt mentioned something about his situation before Richard died."

Edgar, taking in every detail, looked at Miller:

"It looks like we're due for another round of questions."

Drake and Miller, having gathered all the materials they'd collected, made their way to Oliver, hoping he could shed light on Hunt's last meetings or words. They found him in the library, where he greeted them with a cautious look.

"Oliver," Edgar began calmly, "there's one detail that puzzles us. Just how close were Hunt and Richard? And what kind of ties did Hunt have with the family?"

Oliver seemed to drift into thought, his gaze unfocused as if revisiting distant memories.

"In fact, Hunt wasn't a frequent guest here," he began. "Father and Uncle Richard met with him strictly on business matters, and these meetings were always held in the office or at their firms. It wasn't something family-related. But the week before Uncle's death, I noticed they were meeting again. Hunt wasn't his usual self; he seemed nervous, pacing the room and looking at Uncle Richard in a… threatening way."

Miller and Edgar exchanged a look, realizing these talks may have gone beyond professional dealings.

"And anything else?" Miller asked. "Perhaps you overheard some part of their conversation or noticed other details?"

Oliver nodded, his face turning pale.

"Not everything, but I did hear Hunt say, 'You promised me your commitments.'" Oliver continued, choosing his words as if replaying the memory in his mind.

"My uncle replied something along the lines of, 'I fulfilled my part and owe you nothing more.' Hunt looked… furious, almost desperate. I'm not sure of the specifics, but there was a clear hint of threat in his tone. As I slipped away from the door to avoid being noticed, the last thing I heard was Hunt saying, 'If you can't fulfill your promise, I'll make you pay in my own way.'"

Drake and Miller silently absorbed this, understanding the situation went deeper than unsettled financial matters.

"It sounds like Hunt was certain he held some leverage over Richard," Edgar said quietly. "Maybe he knew something incriminating."

Miller frowned.

"If that's the case, it means Hunt was blackmailing Richard and was prepared to take drastic action if he didn't comply."

Oliver nodded, his face becoming more serious.

"I think that's why my uncle started talking about the 'keys' he'd leave behind. He was troubled. This wasn't just business or debt; it seemed like Hunt was threatening his family or reputation."

Drake and Miller realized the situation was intensifying.

"Thank you, Oliver. Your help is indeed invaluable," Edgar said, standing. "Now we have another lead to investigate."

After Oliver left, Miller turned to Edgar.

"If Hunt was threatening not only Richard but his family, that could be a motive for murder. And someone who knew about his intentions might have decided to eliminate him before he could act on his threats."

Edgar nodded thoughtfully.

"The question remains: who might have been helping Hunt within the household? It seems we have another target for surveillance tonight."

Late at night, after their rounds, Drake and Miller settled into their positions to keep watch. They arranged themselves in a small recess at the end of the hallway, from where they had a clear view of the approach to the study. Their "cover" was made up of two stools hastily taken from a nearby room, allowing them to sit in the shadows, hidden from sight.

"Certain someone needs this more than anyone else here," Miller whispered, quietly tugging off his gloves to catch every possible detail.

"Yeah," Edgar replied softly, making himself comfortable. "If they make a move, they must think it'll be easy to fool us."

Time crawled by as the mansion grew silent around them. Drake and Miller waited patiently, listening intently to every sound, exchanging brief words about plans in case someone appeared. Around midnight, as the night was at its darkest and sleep almost overtook them both, a faint light flickered at the end of the hallway.

Edgar tensed, catching movement, and motioned to Miller to look at the light. The flashlight beam was moving slowly and cautiously toward the study where Simon's laptop with the hidden files was kept.

"That him?" Miller whispered, leaning slightly forward.

"Let's not reveal ourselves just yet," Edgar whispered back, not taking his eyes off the light.

They remained tense as the figure, sensing something, suddenly froze. An absolute silence followed, then the figure dashed toward the nearest window. Both men jumped up, restraining their impulse to charge forward, and watched as the stranger swung the window open and leapt outside.

Reaching the window, Edgar strained to make out the figure's direction as it vanished into the shadows of the garden trees.

"They're gone," Miller whispered, frustrated. "But if it was someone from the house, they may have already returned to their room."

"We'll split up," Edgar agreed, already heading toward the staircase. "Check everyone."

They moved through the house, checking each room, but all the residents appeared to be in their beds, either asleep or feigning surprise at being awakened by sudden noise. When they finally reached Amelia's room, Edgar stopped, eyeing the windowsill suspiciously. A faint streak of dirt ran along the surface, as if someone had recently leaned against the frame to open the window.

"Miller, look at this," Edgar pointed at the windowsill, his gaze cautious. "These marks… What do you think?"

Miller stepped closer, examining the dirt on the windowsill.

"It's definitely from outside," he replied thoughtfully. "Either someone went out or came back in."

Edgar nodded, continuing to stare intently into the night beyond the window.

"It doesn't look like an accident. Either it's her tracks, or someone's trying to frame her."

They stood in silence, thinking over what they'd seen. The mansion returned to stillness, but the signs were clear: their investigation was taking a new, increasingly sinister turn.

Drake and Miller exchanged glances, silently contemplating the recent events. The dirt on Amelia's windowsill clearly indicated that someone had either tried to break in or escape through her window.

"It looks like it's time we spoke with Amelia," Miller whispered, keeping his voice low enough not to wake the others.

"Agreed, but first, let's confirm whether this was a setup," Edgar replied, gesturing to the fresh mark on the windowsill. "Someone may be trying to lead us astray."

They decided to leave the matter for the morning to avoid raising any alarms in the house. Returning to their posts, Drake and Miller took a thorough walk around the property, checking windows and doors to make sure everything was locked and that no additional signs of forced entry were present.

They barely slept that night. At dawn, as the mansion began to wake, they were prepared for the upcoming conversation.

When Amelia came down for breakfast, Edgar pulled her aside, his tone calm and casual.

"Amelia, could you help us with something? We've noticed a few odd details and wondered if you'd noticed anything unusual recently."

Her face briefly registered concern, but she quickly composed herself and replied, "No, nothing like that… although I did notice someone might have been in my room recently. A few things were out of place. I thought it was you two," she added, her voice tinged with mild tension.

Edgar exchanged a glance with Miller, taking note of her reaction. Each word could be a clue, and they knew one wrong step might change everything.

"I understand," Edgar replied softly. "Do you remember when you first noticed someone had been in your room?"

Amelia looked away, seeming to replay the past few days in her mind.

"Honestly, it was last night," she finally said. "I just noticed a little bit of dirt near the window. But I hadn't opened it since yesterday morning."

"Interesting," Miller said, studying her expression. "Didn't it worry you that someone might have used the window?"

Amelia narrowed her eyes as though weighing something.

"Of course it did. I just assumed you were already aware and didn't want to interfere. I know you're investigating," she added, seeming to justify her silence.

Miller and Edgar shared another glance. Amelia's words could mean she knew more than she was letting on or could be a red herring. Edgar decided to adjust his approach.

"Thank you for your help, Amelia. But it's in your best interest to tell us everything you've noticed. This isn't a routine investigation, as you understand. Even the smallest detail might be decisive."

Amelia nodded, a flicker of tension crossing her face. She seemed to hesitate before speaking.

"Well, if you insist… I did hear someone moving around the house at night. The footsteps were quiet, like they were trying to go unnoticed. It struck me as strange, but I...," she trailed off, "assumed it was one of you."

Miller listened intently, then leaned closer to Edgar and whispered, "It might be worth checking not only the rooms but also the external cameras. If someone broke in, there should be a record."

Edgar nodded. They thanked Amelia and left, firmly resolved to examine all available footage. Somewhere in this mansion lay the key to unraveling this mystery, and it was time to find it.

They made their way down the corridor toward the surveillance room, where the monitors were kept. Edgar had a strong hunch that tonight might bring something significant, and he hurried forward.

Miller looked around cautiously to ensure they weren't being followed. The silence in the house seemed to deepen with each step, as if the very atmosphere was brimming with tension.

"I think someone's feeling pretty confident that we're not seeing everything," Miller said. "Otherwise, they wouldn't leave traces that could give them away."

They entered the dimly lit surveillance room, and Edgar turned on the monitors. They observed several camera angles, switching between them until one of the nighttime recordings caught movement by Amelia's window.

The screen showed someone dressed in dark clothing. The person moved carefully toward Amelia's window, paused, glanced around, then attempted to open the frame. After a moment, they seemed to reconsider and disappeared into the shadows.

"See that?" Miller whispered, his eyes glued to the screen. "We have a recording."

Edgar frowned, analyzing what he'd seen.

"Looks like they intended to break in but may have noticed us or someone else," he speculated. "Well, now we know where to look next."

Miller nodded.

"Maybe it's time to check in with the others, see if they're all right."

Drake and Miller silently left the monitoring room, considering how best to approach the next steps. If the person in the recording was their main suspect, they were now closer to uncovering some kind of scheme. Only one question remained—who in the house was helping Hunt, and who else might have benefitted from this secretive visit.

As they made their way to the residents' rooms, they passed by the hallway leading to Amelia's room. Miller paused, carefully examining the floor near her door, then knocked, gesturing to Edgar that they should perhaps step inside to check.

"We'll be in only briefly, just to make sure everything is in order," Miller whispered as he opened the door.

The room was tidy and empty, but as soon as they stepped inside, Edgar noticed something on the floor near the window—tiny particles of dirt that seemed to form a trail from the window toward her desk.

"Something was left behind," Edgar whispered, kneeling to examine the odd marks more closely. Miller came nearer, their eyes meeting again.

"It looks like they were searching for something specific. We already saw someone try to enter the room from the outside. I wonder what they hoped to find here," said Miller, scanning the room.

They carefully exited, closing the door behind them. The plan was simple—check the other rooms once more, then gather everyone for a conversation.

The detective and the officer decided to conduct a group conversation with all family members to see if anyone had noticed anything unusual in the past few days. They went to the main hall, where the family typically gathered in the mornings, and asked everyone to join them. Once everyone was seated, Edgar began the conversation.

"We've found something intriguing, and before proceeding, we'd like to ask a few questions," Edgar began, watching the expressions of those present. "In the past few days, has anyone noticed strange sounds, signs, or unexpected visits?"

Lucy, seated next to her brother, nervously glanced at him, then raised her hand.

"A few nights ago, I heard footsteps in the hallway near my room. At first, I thought it was one of you doing a routine check, but the steps were... too slow. As if the person didn't want to be heard."

Edgar nodded, taking note of the detail.

"Anyone else?" he continued, shifting his gaze to Andrew, who looked slightly unsettled.

Andrew coughed lightly and admitted, "Last week, something strange happened in my study as well. The papers on my desk weren't the way I'd left them. I assumed I'd just forgotten, but now... I'm not sure."

Miller listened carefully, then, signaling to Edgar, leaned in to whisper quietly, "It seems like more than one person in the house knows what's going on. Someone here is hiding something or has noticed more than they're letting on."

Edgar turned his attention to Amelia, who was staring at the floor.

"And you, Amelia?" he asked gently, understanding that her answers could prove critical. "Have you noticed anything unusual or... overheard any conversations worth mentioning?"

Amelia raised her eyes, her expression cautious yet determined.

"Actually… yes. But I wanted to be sure it was important. A few days ago, passing by Richard's study, I overheard someone talking about a 'debt' that needed to be 'covered.' The voices were muffled, but it sounded serious."

Drake and Miller listened attentively as Amelia spoke with noticeable apprehension:

"It happened late one evening; I accidentally overheard a phone conversation. The sound was muffled, and I couldn't make out most of the words, but it seemed to be about some kind of obligation, an old matter, something from the past. The voice was low and… strained, as if the person was purposely speaking softly to avoid being overheard."

Edgar nodded thoughtfully, absorbing the details.

"Were you able to catch any key words? Perhaps something that stood out more clearly?" he asked cautiously, hoping to gather just a little more.

Amelia shook her head.

"No, only fragments. But the tone was serious, and the person sounded irritated, as if they didn't want to discuss it but couldn't avoid the topic."

Miller and Edgar exchanged cautious glances. Once they were alone, Miller lowered his voice.

"It sounds like there's something connecting this house to the past. And, judging by her words, it's something no one wants to discuss openly."

Edgar pondered this.

"We should check the remaining records and documents. If this is indeed related to some sort of obligation or debt, it may still be hanging over someone in the family."

The next morning, after gaining access to the call logs, Miller was surprised to discover that, over the past few weeks, numerous calls had been made from the Lancaster residence to the phone number belonging to Maxwell Hunt. And all the records showed the same caller's name—Andrew.

When Edgar reviewed the printout, his expression grew intent.

"It seems Hunt and Andrew were much closer than Andrew let on," Miller noted, watching Edgar's reaction closely.

"And this looks more and more like a conspiracy," Edgar nodded. "We need to make sure there aren't any other clues we might have missed."

Determined to recheck the security camera footage, Edgar now set the video to fast-forward, hoping to catch something that might have slipped by them previously. After a few minutes, he noticed a strange flicker on the screen. Slowing down the video, he saw that the footage momentarily cut out, as if a section had been deleted or masked.

"This flicker appears each time someone exits through the main door," Edgar murmured, showing Miller. "It looks like the cameras are set to skip certain moments."

Miller folded his arms, studying the screen.

"Someone didn't want us knowing when they were coming or going. Either someone in the house pre-edited the footage, or someone on the outside hacked it. But one thing's clear—this was no accident."

Edgar leaned back in his chair, considering their next move.

"We need to check Simon's laptop again. There might be traces of access or modifications that could explain the missing footage."

Miller nodded, and they reopened Simon's laptop. But as soon as they logged into the system, the screen suddenly flashed, and a red skull appeared in the center. The image lingered for a few seconds before disappearing, and then, one by one, all folders and documents began to vanish. Edgar tried pressing keys to halt the process, but nothing worked; each file was systematically erased.

"It's a kill switch virus," Edgar murmured, realizing they'd been outmaneuvered. "The laptop was rigged to delete everything automatically if accessed."

Miller closed the laptop, his face tense.

"We'll hand it over to the specialists. Maybe something can be salvaged. But now it's clear someone knew our intentions and planned for this."

Drake and Miller left the room with the laptop, realizing that someone had pre-set a trap to erase crucial evidence. Despite the loss of data, their resolve to uncover the truth only grew stronger.

They were contemplating their next steps when Miller, deep in thought, remarked:

"We've come too close. Whoever orchestrated all this clearly knows we're getting closer and is trying to erase any remaining traces. Maybe it's time to turn up the pressure and put those hiding the truth on edge."

Edgar nodded, considering the plan.

Chapter 10: Invisible Clues

After the data on Simon's laptop was destroyed, Edgar realized that their opponents were prepared to do anything to cover their tracks. This led him to think about taking extra security measures. To expose the entire scheme and identify those secretly entering the house, he decided to set up hidden surveillance cameras—one outside and another in the study.

Drake got to work that very evening. Under the cover of night, he discreetly installed the first camera at the main entrance. Surrounded by shadows and carefully camouflaged, the camera was positioned to capture anyone approaching or leaving the house while remaining invisible.

Finishing up outside, he returned to the house to set up the second camera in the study. He chose a discreet spot on a shelf near the massive cabinet, positioning the camera to cover the entire room. Now, if anyone tried to enter the study or tamper with evidence again, the recording would capture all the details.

When the cameras were installed and tested, Edgar leaned back in his chair and, checking the footage on his phone, felt a sense of relief: every movement in and around the house would now be securely monitored.

With the new day, Drake and Miller focused on analyzing the data from the new cameras. They agreed not to draw attention to the devices just yet, hoping to avoid scaring off anyone who might approach the house or enter the study.

The day passed in the usual routine at the Lancaster estate, with no incidents, and it was only by late evening that the detectives resumed their surveillance. They took positions in the living room, where they could view footage from the entrance camera on Edgar's phone. Edgar connected his phone to the system, watching the main entrance and tracking any changes, while Miller focused intently on the study in case anyone appeared there.

Around midnight, Edgar noticed a faint movement on the screen. A figure in dark clothing had approached the front door, cautiously looking around before slowly pushing it open. Edgar subtly signaled to Miller, and they both began observing the intruder's actions.

"Looks like we have a visitor," Edgar whispered, keeping his gaze on the screen.

The person on video appeared tense, glancing around as they silently moved down the corridor toward the study. Drake and Miller followed quietly at a distance. Suddenly, the figure halted, as if sensing something, and unexpectedly veered toward the side door that led into the garden.

Drake and Miller continued to tail the stranger, carefully avoiding any noise. When the figure vanished into the garden's shadows, they exchanged a glance, realizing it was time to act decisively.

Drake gestured for Miller to circle around the house from the other side to cut off any possible escape route. Silently, they split up, each moving along their side of the building to keep the stranger in view.

Amidst the thick shadows cast by trees, the stranger paused, as if ensuring they weren't being followed. They crouched and raised a hand to their ear, seemingly whispering into a small device. Edgar managed to get close enough to hear fragments of the words:

"The plan… is on schedule… no one knows…"

But, before finishing, the stranger suddenly straightened and, glancing back, spotted Edgar's shadow. In an instant, they bolted deeper into the garden, and Edgar gave chase. Miller, seeing the movement, sped up around the house to intercept the intruder.

The darkness of the garden, with its winding paths and dense shrubs, made the pursuit challenging. Edgar tried to keep the silhouette in sight, weaving between trees. He nearly caught up to the stranger when they leapt off a small terrace and, grabbing onto a low-hanging branch, swiftly disappeared into the bushes beyond the estate's perimeter.

Drake stopped, just as Miller, breathing heavily from the run, arrived.

"Damn it, they got away again," Miller muttered, scowling at the empty dark pathway.

Edgar nodded silently, disappointed, but, looking back toward the house, noted, "At least we know they're still nearby. Tomorrow, we'll review the camera footage and discuss how to use it."

Their conversation was interrupted by a faint rustling sound from the direction of the house.

Drake and Miller returned inside, listening to the silence that felt almost too tense. They slowly crossed the hall, heading to the room with the equipment to review the camera footage. Edgar played the last file, searching for any minute detail in the intruder's movements.

On the screen, the image showed a dark figure slowly approaching the house, scanning the surroundings as if searching for something or someone. After a few seconds, they stopped and raised a hand to their ear, as though speaking into a hidden device.

Miller frowned, studying the details closely.

"They definitely have an accomplice—someone who's coordinating their actions. It seems they're being more cautious than we expected."

Edgar sighed, realizing that each new step in the investigation raised more questions than it answered.

"We'll need to install an additional camera near the terrace," he replied quietly. "If they try to escape again, we'll have a better chance of catching them on tape."

Miller nodded in agreement.

"We'll set it up tomorrow, and also check the nearby area. If they have contact points, there should be some signs close by."

That night, they went through the entire house once more, double-checking the locks and windows to prevent another break-in. But Edgar's mind was occupied with something else: why would their suspect risk coming back here?

The next morning, as planned, Drake and Miller installed an additional camera by the terrace, carefully camouflaging it among thick bushes. Now, every approach to the house was under surveillance, and they hoped this would be enough to catch any suspicious movements from uninvited guests.

After the setup was complete, Miller decided to examine the nearby grounds for any suspicious traces, while Edgar stayed inside, analyzing footage from the previous night in search of even the slightest sign that might point to the intruder's identity.

As night fell, with all preparations in place, they set up another night watch. Drake and Miller positioned themselves in the living room with access to the cameras, monitoring everything happening inside and around the house. As the minutes ticked by, the tension inside the Lancaster estate grew heavier.

Around 2 a.m., a shadowy figure appeared on the screen, carefully approaching the terrace.

Edgar stiffened, closely watching the figure's movements. The intruder crept towards the house, pausing as though assessing the situation. This time, he was more cautious, avoiding the camera at the main entrance and seemingly heading straight for the study via the terrace.

Miller signaled that he would take the side route to intercept the intruder, while Edgar remained at the monitor, following every move.

The figure reached the study window, quickly glanced around, and, ensuring no one was watching, managed to open it with precision and ease, as if he knew how to bypass the locks. Moments later, he was inside.

Edgar paused, waiting for the camera to capture the intruder's face. However, instead of looking up, the figure immediately moved toward the desk, rifling through the papers. Then, a flicker crossed his face as he glanced in the direction of the camera hidden among the books, as if sensing something.

Suddenly, Miller's voice came through the radio:

"I'm by the study door; is he already inside?"

"Yes," Edgar replied quietly. "Move quickly, before he finds anything."

Miller silently approached the study door and opened it cautiously, listening intently for the slightest sound. The room was empty — the window was open, and the curtains swayed in the night's breeze. Sensing someone's presence, the intruder had fled just moments before Miller entered.

A few minutes later, Drake joined him. They searched the study carefully, examining every item. Edgar's eyes settled on a shelf beside the large leather chair.

"Something's definitely missing here," he said softly, leaning closer to the empty frame on the shelf. "There was a photo of Richard here."

"So that's all he came for," muttered Miller, nodding. "Left in a hurry but didn't leave a trace. Nothing else was touched."

Back at the monitors, they reviewed the study's camera footage. The screen showed the hooded figure in a tightly fitted mask and gloves quickly approaching the window. Edgar examined every movement, but the intruder's identity remained hidden. The only conclusion was that the figure was likely a man.

"He moved with clear purpose," Edgar observed. "He knew exactly what he wanted."

Drake and Miller exchanged thoughtful glances. The loss of Richard's photograph raised questions — as did the fact that the intruder left everything else untouched. Clearly, he knew what he was looking for and was willing to take the risk for that one photo.

"It doesn't seem like just a random visit," Miller said, reviewing the footage again. "The photo might hold some significance we haven't figured out yet."

"Or maybe it's a key to something bigger," Edgar replied, frowning. "Someone might think we could use it to follow their trail. Taking something like this… it feels like they're covering their tracks but making sure we notice."

Miller nodded thoughtfully.

"We still have cameras at the entrance and around the perimeter. Maybe we'll find some clues there."

They began reviewing other footage, and on the camera by the main entrance, the same figure was visible, silently slipping toward the window and disappearing into the shadows of the garden. Edgar paused the recording, scrutinizing the image.

"He deliberately avoided lit areas," he noted. "Moved confidently, as if he knew the layout of the house and exactly where the cameras were."

Miller gave a small, wry smile.

"Someone who knows our setup well and knows this house…"

Edgar thought over his words, then stood up.

"All right, we'll keep monitoring the hidden cameras."

Drake and Miller returned to their posts, contemplating the significance of the missing photograph of Richard. It seemed the photo held some value for the intruder, but why risk breaking into the house for a single picture?

They decided not to raise any alarm, hoping the intruder wouldn't realize he had been noticed. Perhaps, by maintaining an appearance of calm, they could catch him red-handed.

Leaving the cameras active, they chose to shift their focus temporarily to the call records Miller had received that morning. Among Andrew's calls to Hunt's number, they noticed a strange coincidence—one of the calls had been made on the same day the first signs of intrusion appeared in the house.

Edgar pulled up the date of the call on the screen and the camera footage from that day, fast-forwarding to the moment someone had slipped into the house. Once again, the video showed a figure in dark clothing sliding through the garden and quickly disappearing into the shadows.

"I think if we can figure out how they coordinated these intrusions, we might be able to identify their ally," Edgar said quietly, noting the intruder's repeated movements.

At that moment, Miller glanced at the list of calls:

"There are calls that match up with the moments of movement on the cameras. It looks like they used calls as signals to start the break-ins. I wonder if these calls can point us to the intervals when they were planning each new attempt."

Edgar nodded, studying the recordings.

"Let's track them across the camera footage once more and see if any patterns emerge from the most recent recordings."

They began another round of analysis, trying to identify any repeated signals and timing patterns when the intruder might have approached the house again.

As Drake and Miller continued to examine the calls and footage, they hoped to find clues that would lead them to the next step. Time passed, and with each new detail, they felt closer to the truth.

By the middle of the night, they noticed another pattern: one of the calls made a few days ago coincided with the time the intruder had approached the house once again. The dark-clothed figure appeared only briefly, but the footage revealed the figure's movements—the intruder clearly knew how to avoid the cameras and where each surveillance point was located.

Edgar focused intently on the screen, observing the intruder's movements until he finally noticed something that caught his attention:

"Look, Miller. This person isn't just dodging the cameras—they're very familiar with each one. They know all the surveillance spots, which suggests they've been in the house before."

Miller nodded, his expression tense.

"So, this is likely someone who's been here before, someone who knows not only the location of the cameras but also the hidden approaches to the house."

Edgar opened the mansion's floor plan and recalled an old corridor running from the garden straight to the study. It was rarely used and camouflaged among thick shrubs, making it accessible only to those familiar with the grounds.

"I think we should focus on this entrance next time," he said thoughtfully, pointing to the plan. "If the intruder plans another visit, they'll probably use this hidden path."

Miller considered his suggestion and proposed:

"Let's install another hidden camera and motion detectors. If they take this route, we'll spot them before they get anywhere close to the house."

With the arrival of dawn, they set up new equipment and carefully concealed cameras and sensors along the hidden path, hoping this would be the final step in catching the intruder.

They spent the night in tense anticipation, closely monitoring the recordings and screens, keeping watch over every corner of the mansion and its surroundings. Time passed, but, contrary to their expectations, the area around the house remained quiet, and none of the cameras detected any movement.

Their exhaustion finally got the better of them, and around five in the morning, with the night coming to an end, they both drifted off in the sitting room. The strain of constant vigilance, which had kept them on edge for days, slowly overtook them.

Through the calm of the early morning, a loud scream suddenly cut through the air at seven. Both detectives sprang to their feet, instantly alert, and rushed towards the sound.

The scream came from the upper floor, where Evelyn's room was located. As they approached, they heard Lucy standing in the doorway, pale with terror, calling for help:

"Mom! Someone, help! She... she isn't moving!"

Drake and Miller rushed to the door and saw Evelyn lying on the bed with her eyes closed, motionless and pale. Lucy stood nearby, gripping the edge of the bed, trying to bring her mother to consciousness.

"Please, tell me she'll be alright! She's not responding," her voice trembled.

Miller gently moved Lucy aside, allowing the doctor, who had been called a few minutes later, to examine Evelyn. The doctor carefully checked her pulse, observed her closely, and with a concerned look, finally sighed and said:

"She's experiencing severe exhaustion and nervous strain. Right now, she urgently needs bed rest and complete tranquility. If her condition doesn't improve, she'll need hospitalization."

Exchanging glances, Drake and Miller decided to inspect the room after the doctor left. The first thing Edgar noticed was a pair of shoes poking out from under the bed. Picking one up, he saw fresh dirt on them, as though someone had recently worn them outside.

Another odd detail was that these shoes appeared to be larger than Evelyn's usual size. Her other pair—her indoor slippers—stood nearby, and these were clearly much smaller. Edgar shook his head as he examined them, murmuring:

"Either someone took these by accident, or they left them here on purpose."

Miller frowned and pointed at a teacup on the nightstand:

"One more thing: she left her tea almost untouched, only slightly sipped. I think we should examine its contents."

Edgar nodded in agreement:

"Miller, send a sample of this liquid for testing. It might be crucial, perhaps even the key to her current state."

They returned to Lucy, comforting her and carefully explaining that she needed to let her mother rest and follow the doctor's instructions closely.

As they left Evelyn's room and descended into the living room, Miller turned to Edgar.

"It seems that everything points to someone in this house persistently hiding more than just family secrets. Much suggests that someone has been closely watching Lucy's mother, and that may have driven her to exhaustion," he said, considering their next steps.

Drake frowned, realizing that the situation might be spiraling out of control.

"If that's the case, then maybe we'll find traces in the kitchen or other rooms. The tea is just part of the story—we need more clues that could confirm these suspicions."

Miller nodded in agreement.

"Additionally, it wouldn't hurt to check if there are any items in the house belonging to whoever might have used her shoes or tried entering her room. If our intruder is one of the household, there should be something around here."

Chapter 11: Concealed Traces

In search of potential leads, Drake and Miller headed to the kitchen, where the head housekeeper, Martha, supervised the meals and upkeep of the house. They approached her directly but cautiously.

"Martha, Mrs. Evelyn asked for tea in her room last night. Could you tell us who brought it up?" Edgar asked.

"Usually, it's either me or Miss Lucy, but last night Evelyn asked for privacy. The tea was left at her door, and she took it herself," Martha replied, slightly flustered.

Edgar noted that Lucy, according to Martha, often brought tea to her mother, and decided to keep this in mind, careful not to overlook any small detail. They returned to the living room and reviewed the updated camera footage, hoping the intruder wouldn't take the risk of returning so soon after his last visit.

They also kept an eye on the behavior of the other family members, suspecting that one of them might have been helping this person.

Drake and Miller continued observing everyone's behavior throughout the day, but by nightfall, nothing suspicious had come to light. As night fell, they resumed their positions, careful not to miss any movement near the estate.

All was quiet until about two in the morning, when a shadowy figure cautiously crept up to the house. The intruder, avoiding the camera angles, stealthily made his way to the terrace and slipped inside, heading straight for the study.

Once he was in the study, Edgar signaled to Miller. Miller silently approached the door and entered, catching the intruder in the act. The figure in dark clothing froze for a moment, then slowly raised his hands to his face and removed his mask, calmly looking at Miller. It was Thomas.

"I know you have questions," Thomas said quietly. "The answer may be here," he indicated a photograph of Richard in his hand. "At first, I thought it was just a keepsake of him, but on the back, I discovered encoded symbols."

Edgar entered and closed the door behind him.

"So you were looking for the key to the cipher here, in the study?" he asked, keeping his tone neutral.

Thomas nodded.

"Yes. The photo has a reference to the chimney damper. If I'm right, it could help decipher my father's message."

Drake, Miller, and Thomas stood by the fireplace, examining the hidden compartment behind the panel. Carefully shifting it aside, Edgar uncovered a small envelope placed within the niche. Unfolding it, he pulled out two items: a folded paper with a cipher and an old childhood photograph of Thomas. On the back of the photo, there was an inscription: "Please accept him into the family. I never had the courage to do it myself."

Thomas held his breath, gazing at the photograph, then looked over to Edgar, who had already begun to unfold the cipher.

"This code seems to match what's written on the back of Richard's photograph," Edgar said quietly, and they quickly moved to the desk to begin deciphering it.

The complex pattern of letters gradually revealed a coherent message. They sat in silence at the desk, each focusing on the cipher sheet. Edgar, cross-referencing the writing on the back of the photograph, started matching the sequence of symbols. Thomas watched his hands closely, while Miller periodically glanced at the door, straining to detect any sound that might indicate someone approaching.

The cipher was challenging, but after a few minutes, the message started to make sense.

"In the long walls of this house, the truth about those who played their game is hidden," Edgar read aloud. "Behind the beam in the library lies what will put an end to these manipulations."

Thomas, grasping the significance, nodded tensely.

"So, the whole truth is there — hidden, but within reach."

Wasting no time, they headed to the library.

Drake, Miller, and Thomas entered the library, scanning the room to avoid missing anything that could lead them to the concealed location. The room had several beams, and they decided to inspect each one methodically.

The first beam yielded nothing, as did the second. Finally, reaching the third beam, Thomas felt his fingers brush against a barely perceptible gap.

"There's something here," he whispered, glancing over at Drake and Miller.

Thomas carefully pressed the edge of the beam, and soon a small compartment opened within. Inside was an envelope with a flash drive.

"Found something?" Miller whispered, leaning in.

"Looks like a flash drive," Thomas replied, pulling it out and showing it to Drake and Miller.

Satisfied the room was empty and they were still undetected, Edgar nodded toward the door.

"We need to see what's on this drive. This could be exactly what we're looking for."

They headed to Miller's room, where he provided his own laptop. Edgar inserted the flash drive, and its contents popped up on the screen. Several folders appeared, with names such as "Correspondence," "Documents," "Debt Records," and "Reports."

"This looks like the key to exposing Hunt," said Miller, exchanging a quick glance with Edgar.

In one of the folders, they found detailed documents confirming Hunt's fraudulent schemes, forged debt obligations, data falsifications, and correspondence with unnamed associates discussing plans to exert pressure on the Lancasters.

"This is an entire web of deception," Miller muttered as he browsed through the documents. "Hunt wasn't just forging a debt; he was building a plan to control the Lancasters and siphon money from them."

Thomas, standing a little aside, kept his eyes on the screen, observing every detail. Suddenly, his attention was caught by correspondence signed with the initials "R.L.," possibly his father Richard.

"That's Richard's signature," Thomas whispered. "Did he know about Hunt's schemes?"

Edgar frowned, understanding the possible implications of this discovery.

"I doubt he was in on it. More likely, Hunt was threatening or attempting to blackmail him to conceal his own financial instability," Edgar suggested.

As they continued scanning the records, Edgar came across an encrypted letter in which Hunt mentioned an important document kept in the Lancaster household, related to one of the debt agreements.

Edgar opened the encrypted file, but a code blocked access — the message was clearly hidden behind a complex encryption. Thomas, keeping his gaze fixed on the screen, murmured:

"Maybe this is what my father referred to in the note on the photograph. The cipher we found behind the panel might be the key."

Edgar nodded, realizing that without decoding it, they wouldn't be able to fully understand Hunt's role in the financial schemes or the extent of his influence over the Lancasters.

"If we apply the cipher correctly, it should give us access to the file," Miller said thoughtfully, inserting the text from the envelope they had found earlier.

After a few minutes of entering the cipher and testing combinations, the file finally opened. The screen displayed documents from several years ago, with headings indicating Hunt's illegal financial dealings and the forged debts he'd manufactured against the Lancasters. But among the various papers, one note captured Edgar's attention. It read:

"If things turn dangerous for me, all obligations pass to a new heir through Mary, if she remains the only link between the families."

"It seems Hunt anticipated that his manipulations might be exposed," Edgar remarked. "In that case, his debt would shift onto the Lancasters through Mary, binding the family even more."

Thomas paled, realizing that his mother might have been the link Hunt was leveraging in his schemes.

Thomas ran a hand over his face, trying to process these new details.

"So, Hunt planned to use my mother all along, even after things became risky," he said, his voice filled with confusion. "That explains why she sometimes looked so burdened, like something was weighing heavily on her."

Edgar nodded, considering everything he had just heard.

"He likely pressured her, convincing her of his influence and importance. The debt became the tool he intended to use to keep the Lancasters bound to him, regardless of the outcome."

Miller, quickly scanning the documents on the screen, paused at one of the letters. Signed with Hunt's initials, it mentioned a "final step" to compel Richard to fulfill their agreement. This letter was dated just a day before Richard's sudden death.

"He must have moved to more drastic measures when he realized Richard wouldn't continue supporting his plans," Miller remarked. "It seems like the pressure intensified, and this 'final step' took its toll."

Thomas clenched his fists, realizing the full extent of Hunt's actions. If Hunt had truly planned this kind of trap for the family, without regard for sacrifices, who might have been his next target?

Edgar looked closely at the screen, where names and addresses of unknown contacts involved in Hunt's communications appeared.

"We need to find out who among these people might have been his ally. It's possible some of them are still connected to the house and could confirm or refute this theory," concluded Edgar, saving the contact list into a separate file.

Thomas, shaken by the flood of emotions, nodded, trying to absorb everything he had just heard.

"We'll review these contacts," Edgar said, glancing over at Thomas, "but for now, it's essential to keep all of this confidential. Our goal is to determine if any other Lancasters or Hunt's acquaintances are involved and if any of them are connected to recent events in the house."

Thomas remained silent, digesting the information, and finally asked quietly:

"If my mother was somehow involved in his plans, does that mean she was helping him? Or did Hunt simply use her to get control over our family?"

Miller placed a hand on his shoulder.

"That's exactly what we intend to find out. Based on these documents, Hunt planned this well in advance to keep a hold on the Lancasters. But his actions were driven by fear and desperation, and he didn't foresee that they'd lead to serious consequences."

Edgar reopened the document folder and stumbled upon a file marked with the initial "M." It referenced Mary and contained specific instructions on transferring financial assets.

"This mentions that all of Hunt's assets should go into her control in the event of his death. He clearly didn't plan to let his debts go unpaid without some gain," Edgar noted, looking over at Thomas. "It seems he wanted to bind your family so that even after his death, the Lancasters would still be indebted to him."

They exchanged contemplative looks.

"Thomas," Miller added, "if any memories come to mind—any details about those Hunt kept in contact with—now's the time to share. Even a small recollection could clarify his intentions."

Thomas paused, concentrating on the list of names. He scanned it, then frowned.

"I don't recognize most of these names, but I definitely heard a few of them before, when I happened to overhear Hunt talking to my mother. He seemed familiar with these people, though he never brought them to the house. But one of them had a nickname—something like 'North.' I heard it several times but didn't think it was anything serious."

Edgar took note of this and then looked over at Miller.

"We need to check that nickname and see if it matches any of these contacts. There might be a key player in Hunt's network hiding behind it."

Miller nodded and began searching on his laptop.

Thomas took a deep breath, processing everything he had heard:

"If this is somehow tied to inheritance or debts, does that mean I'm the heir Hunt intended to tie to the Lancasters?"

Edgar, Miller, and Thomas stood by the fireplace, studying the hidden space behind the grate. Carefully moving it aside, Edgar discovered an envelope tucked into the niche. Opening it, he pulled out two items: a folded sheet with a cipher and an old childhood photograph of Thomas. On the back of the photo was written, "Please accept him into the family. I was too cowardly to do it in time."

Holding his breath, Thomas looked at the photograph, then at Edgar, who had already started unfolding the ciphered sheet.

"This cipher appears to match the one written on the back of Richard's photograph," Edgar murmured, and they immediately sat down to begin the decryption process.

As the intricate pattern of symbols began to reveal itself, they leaned over the table in complete silence, each one focusing on the page. Edgar carefully matched the characters, piecing together a coherent message as Thomas watched closely, and Miller kept an ear out for any sign of movement.

— "Hidden within these walls lies the truth about those who played their game," Edgar read aloud. "Look behind the beam in the library to find what will end their manipulations."

Thomas, realizing the significance, nodded tensely.

— "So the whole truth is there—hidden, but within reach."

Without wasting any time, they headed to the library.

Once inside, Edgar, Miller, and Thomas inspected the room, making sure not to overlook anything that might indicate a concealed hiding spot. The room had several beams, so they decided to check each one in turn.

The first beam held nothing, nor did the second. Finally, reaching the third beam, Thomas felt a slight gap beneath his fingers.

— "There's something here," he whispered, looking at Drake and Miller.

Thomas pressed down on the edge of the beam, and a small compartment opened. Inside, there was a small envelope containing a flash drive.

— "You've found something?" Miller whispered, leaning closer.

— "It looks like a flash drive," Thomas replied, holding up the item for Drake and Miller to see.

After making sure the room was empty and that no one was watching, Edgar nodded toward the door.

— "We need to see what's on this flash drive while we have the chance."

They went to Miller's room, where his laptop was set up. Plugging in the flash drive, Edgar opened its contents. Several folders appeared on the screen, labeled "Correspondence," "Documents," "Debt Notes," and "Reports."

— "Looks like this could be the key to exposing Hunt's schemes," Miller said, exchanging a glance with Edgar.

In one folder, they found detailed documents confirming Hunt's fraudulent schemes, falsified debt obligations, tampered data, and correspondence with unidentified contacts, discussing plans to put pressure on the Lancasters.

Thomas, standing nearby, tensely followed the details on the screen. His attention was drawn to a correspondence signed with the initials "R.L.," which could point to Richard Lancaster.

— "That's Richard's signature," Thomas said quietly. "Did he know about Hunt's manipulations?"

Edgar frowned, grasping the potential implications.

— "I doubt he was involved. More likely, Hunt tried to blackmail him or manipulate him into covering up his financial instability," Edgar suggested.

As they continued reading, Edgar suddenly came across an encrypted letter in which Hunt mentioned an important document stored in the Lancaster home, tied to one of the debt obligations.

Opening the encrypted file, Edgar encountered an unknown code—it was clearly hidden behind a complex encryption system. Without looking up, Thomas muttered:

— "Maybe this is what my father mentioned in the note on the photo. The cipher we found behind the grate might be the key."

Edgar nodded, realizing that without decryption, they couldn't uncover the extent of Hunt's influence over the Lancasters.

— "If we can crack this code, we might gain full access to the file," Miller said thoughtfully, inputting text from the cipher they'd discovered.

After a few minutes of entering the code and trying different combinations, the file finally opened. The screen displayed documents dating back several years, revealing Hunt's illegal financial dealings and forged debt obligations against the Lancasters. But among the papers, Edgar found one note that caught his attention. It read:

— "In the event of any refusal to comply, sanctions will be imposed upon the Lancasters. This wasn't just about leaving debt—it was his way to ensure the family would be forced to deal with his artificial 'legacy,'" Edgar muttered.

Miller, choosing his words carefully, turned to Thomas.

— "If you remember anything that could hint at who might have been involved in his schemes, tell us now. We need to identify any partners who might want to continue his plans."

Realizing Hunt's intentions, Drake and Miller began planning how to expose his schemes to the authorities.

— "If Hunt really intended to leave the Lancasters with fake debts, he likely found someone in the house to help monitor them," Miller said, shuffling through the documents again.

Thomas focused on the screen, trying to comprehend how his family was connected to these plans.

— "If my mother was somehow involved in this," he said quietly, "maybe she was under Hunt's pressure. He could've threatened her reputation or exploited an old fear."

Edgar nodded, thinking it through.

— "It's likely Hunt knew Mary felt vulnerable," he said. "Perhaps he convinced her that her future—and yours—depended on his so-called protection. That would explain her unease and anxiety in recent months."

At that moment, Miller spotted a letter among the documents addressed to Mary, warning her about the "need to trust only close associates." At the end of the letter was the alias: North—one of the names Thomas had mentioned earlier.

— "Looks like 'North' does play a significant role," Miller said, showing the letter to Edgar. "He might be one of Hunt's assigned overseers."

Thomas frowned, studying the signature.

— "So, 'North' could be either one of his accomplices or a hired hand," he suggested. "But if he's connected to the house, he must have been watching over us."

Edgar closed the laptop, contemplating their next move.

— "We need to try to contact this 'North.' Hunt probably managed operations from a distance, but judging by his letters, 'North' might be closer to the estate than we thought."

Miller proposed reviewing all recent surveillance footage to check for any suspicious activity that might confirm this unknown observer's presence near the house.

Thomas took a deep breath, absorbing everything he'd heard, then rose to leave.

— "Thomas," Edgar said quietly, "keep all of this to yourself. No one should know what you've seen or heard today."

Thomas nodded, understanding that secrecy was his only way to help the investigation. Moving carefully to avoid drawing attention, he left the room, leaving the detectives to their discoveries and next steps.

Drake and Miller returned to the monitoring room and began fast-forwarding through the recordings, focusing on every minor detail. They felt they were close to identifying "North" if he had indeed been around the house.

After a while, Miller slowed down the footage, pointing to strange movement at the edge of the garden, leading toward the back of the estate.

— "Look," he whispered, pointing to the screen. "Someone's carefully moving toward the terrace."

The figure stayed hidden among the trees and seemed aware of the camera placements, avoiding direct angles. Drake and Miller exchanged glances—this could be "North" or one of Hunt's associates.

— "It looks like he's coming back," Edgar noted. "If 'North' is a frequent visitor, we need to confront him directly."

They decided to set a trap that night, concealing cameras and installing new motion sensors near the rear entrance and the garden. Once again, Drake and Miller positioned themselves in the living room, ready to respond at the slightest movement, and waited tensely for "North" to reappear.

At around two in the morning, a shadowy figure appeared on the monitor, cautiously approaching the mansion. Moving quietly, the figure stayed hidden in the shadows, clearly aware of the cameras' placements. Drake and Miller, already on edge, watched as the intruder crept along the garden walls, deliberately evading the camera angles.

When the figure finally neared the back entrance, Miller activated the motion sensors, and both he and Edgar silently took up positions on either side of the door. The figure glanced around once more and, with a practiced hand, used a lock pick to enter. The movements were fluid, as if this person had done this before.

Drake gave a slight nod to Miller, and as soon as the intruder stepped inside, they closed the door behind him and turned on their flashlights, casting beams straight into the intruder's face. He froze, hands raised.

"Who are you, and what do you want here?" Edgar demanded, his flashlight fixed firmly on the man's face.

The man lowered his hands calmly and, with a steady voice, replied, "Victor Norrington. I believe you're already familiar with my name."

Drake and Miller exchanged wary glances. Norrington's name had come up in Hunter's files on the flash drive, but they hadn't expected to meet him in person.

"Yes, we know who you are. And we know you were close to Hunter. But why are you here?" Edgar asked, watching Norrington's every move.

"Breaking into a house isn't without consequences," Miller added, his tone stern.

Norrington smiled faintly, stepping back with his hands raised in a placating gesture. "Take it easy, gentlemen," he said with a hint of mockery. "I'm not here to break the law; I'm here to talk. I think we have some common interests."

Drake and Miller looked at each other, their suspicion evident. Keeping his tone neutral, Edgar gestured for him to continue.

"Common interests?" Edgar repeated, his expression serious. "We're well aware that Hunter used you to try to control the Lankaster family. And now, if I understand correctly, you plan to continue his work?"

Norrington nodded, sizing up the detectives. "Exactly," he said, his voice steady with confidence. "Hunter had ideas, sure, but he didn't know how to carry them out. I do. And if the Lankasters want freedom from his financial obligations, I'll need to ensure the agreement is honored."

"The debts have nothing to do with you," Miller replied firmly. "Any games you were playing with him ended when the family settled their accounts."

Norrington shook his head with a sardonic smile. "Ah, how naive. That's only how it looks on the surface. Richard left plenty unfinished," he said, fixing his gaze on Edgar, his eyes flashing. "If you're so sure the Lankasters are debt-free, then you don't know their history very well."

Edgar, sensing there might be some truth to his words, probed further. "What exactly are you offering?"

Norrington looked at them, his expression turning colder. "It's a simple offer. You walk away and hand over all the documents you've got. In return, I'll ensure that no harm comes to the family."

Miller's face tightened. "What exactly do you need?" he asked.

"The financial records of the Lankaster family," Norrington replied. "Surely you have Hunter's correspondence with Richard. Hand them over, and this debt won't surface again."

Edgar held his ground, his expression unwavering. "These documents expose Hunter's illegal schemes. Are you suggesting we turn a blind eye and simply hand over all the evidence?"

Norrington shrugged, remaining composed. "Perhaps that's the only way to free the Lankasters. Or do you want them caught in an even deeper mess?"

Edgar's gaze narrowed. "So, you believe you have the right to decide the family's fate? Who gave you that authority? Hunter?"

Norrington chuckled, as if the whole situation was simply amusing to him. "Not Hunter or anyone else. It's just business, gentlemen. Hunter knew that when things got intense, he'd need leverage to keep control. His plans were, in fact, to secure their future—even if it was far from transparent."

"How does that justify breaking and entering?" Miller asked pointedly. "You're not here for the documents, are you? There's something else you want?"

Norrington paused briefly, then replied, "I'm here for one document in particular. If you cooperate, the family will be free from obligations they're not even aware of."

Edgar considered this carefully. "We don't bargain with evidence, but if what you're saying is true, we'll go over the documents thoroughly. The Lankasters won't be pawns in your schemes."

Norrington straightened, seeing they weren't swayed. His face returned to its calm expression. "Are you sure this is the road you want to take? Some doors, once opened, can't be closed."

With that, he turned toward the door, leaving Drake and Miller to reflect on what dark hold might still loom over the Lankaster family.

Chapter 12: New Revelations

Drake and Miller, still reflecting on their meeting with Norrington, decided to check if the specialists had managed to recover Simon's laptop. The next morning, they contacted the lab and soon received news: the laptop was partially restored, along with some encrypted files. Drake and Miller picked up the computer, eager to investigate what information might still be hiding there.

Returning to the house, they went straight to the study and turned on the laptop to examine its contents. Among the recovered files were various documents and several notes left by Simon. One file particularly caught their attention. It mentioned "special arrangements" and, at the end, included the name Victor Norrington.

"It seems Norrington was part of a larger plan," Edgar noted, studying the document. "He might not just be Hunt's partner but someone who's running his own game."

Miller nodded thoughtfully. "We need to learn more about their connections. This document could be useful leverage if Norrington continues to pose a threat to the Lancasters."

At the same time, Evelyn's condition was gradually improving. She was finally allowed out of bed and was beginning to regain her strength, though she still seemed frail. Drake and Miller decided to take advantage of this opportunity to question her about Norrington.

They invited her to the sitting room and, ensuring that she felt comfortable, began their conversation.

"Evelyn, we know that your husband had dealings with a man named Victor Norrington," Edgar began, carefully observing her reaction. "Did you ever meet him?"

Evelyn frowned slightly and, after a brief pause, nodded with difficulty.

"He visited the house once when Richard was still alive… They locked themselves in the study and talked for a long time. Richard looked distressed afterward but didn't want to talk about it with me." She paused, covering her face with her hand, as if the memory caused her pain. "I felt… there was something threatening about that man," she added softly.

Drake and Miller exchanged wary glances, realizing that this shadowy figure, Victor Norrington, had not only been aware of Richard's affairs but might have been manipulating him.

While they were questioning Evelyn, the doctor arrived, interrupting the conversation as Evelyn's condition began to worsen. She asked to be left alone, tired from reliving old memories, and the doctor insisted that she needed complete rest.

When Drake and Miller returned to the study, they received a call informing them that the results of the analysis of Evelyn's teacup were ready. The test revealed a substance capable of causing chronic weakness and exhaustion.

"They were trying to weaken her," Miller concluded. "To keep her out of the way and avoid questions. It explains why she couldn't resist Hunt's plans or the influence of those around him."

Edgar nodded, realizing just how dangerous the game around the Lancasters had become.

"So, there's someone with access to the house who's involved in poisoning her. Now, we need to find out who among them could be connected to Norrington or his associates."

Their investigation was growing increasingly tense, and they understood that their task was not only to expose Hunt's financial schemes but also to unravel a conspiracy that had kept the Lancasters ensnared.

To identify who in the house might be linked to Norrington and complicit in what happened to Evelyn, Drake and Miller decided to install hidden cameras throughout the house. They carefully concealed the devices, making sure no one would suspect their presence, placing them opposite the rooms of each resident, as well as in main hallways, the living room, the study, the kitchen, and even in the utility room.

By morning, they had completed the setup and tested the cameras. Now they had a full view of movements and conversations happening in the mansion, which could reveal who was involved in Evelyn's poisoning or the schemes orchestrated by Hunt and his associates.

After setting up the cameras, Drake and Miller went to the monitoring room, where they could view the footage on multiple screens. The monitors displayed images from different areas of the mansion, allowing them to observe the movements and behavior of everyone in the house.

Soon, the official laboratory results for Evelyn's tea were in. The report indicated the presence of a sedative, known for causing drowsiness and severe fatigue. Reading the report, Edgar frowned.

"That explains her recent symptoms," he said quietly. "Someone wanted to keep her sedated, maybe so she wouldn't notice something important."

Miller considered this. "Possibly to prevent her from saying something vital. We should question her about Norrington and recent events, but carefully—not too much pressure in her current state."

They went to Evelyn's room again, where a nurse and Lucy were attending to her. Evelyn looked a bit better, though still tired. Edgar approached her, gently asking with subtlety:

"Evelyn, we understand your health concerns, but we need to ask a few questions that might help our investigation. You mentioned someone coming into your room when you weren't feeling well. Can you recall who it was?"

Evelyn seemed to strain, as if trying to focus on the memory.

"I remember... a voice," she whispered, looking away. "But everything was foggy. The only thing I heard clearly... was the name 'North.' He wanted something from the Lancasters, but I didn't understand what. He'd been here before with Richard, and I... felt uncomfortable around him. He seemed connected to Hunt and his business."

Drake and Edgar exchanged glances, realizing that Norrington might have visited her with a specific goal.

"Thank you for your memories; this could be helpful. Rest now, and if anything else comes to mind, please let us know," Edgar said as he stood up.

Drake and Miller, still pondering their encounter with Norrington, decided to check the security footage to see if he had been spotted around the house recently. As they scanned through the recordings,

Amelia appeared on screen, her voice soft and excited as she spoke on her phone.

"I miss you, my love..." Amelia's voice was filled with tenderness as she smiled. "Soon... yes, of course."

Drake and Miller exchanged looks, noting the intimate tone of her words. It was clear this wasn't just a friendly call.

"Looks like we have another unknown player in the mix," Miller murmured.

"Yes, but who is he, and why is she hiding him?" Edgar added, keeping his eyes on the screen. "We'll follow up on this later."

Then the camera captured a scene with Andrew and Thomas standing opposite each other in the living room. The atmosphere was slightly tense but respectful. Andrew extended his hand.

"Thomas," he began, looking him directly in the eyes, "I can see the resemblance... You do look like Richard—your face, your stance. I have no reason to doubt that you're his son."

They shook hands briefly, and Andrew added, "That means you're my younger brother."

Thomas nodded slightly, still visibly uncomfortable with the formality of it all.

"Thank you, Andrew. This is... new to me too, but I think time will help us all adjust."

Andrew's expression softened, and he placed a reassuring hand on Thomas's shoulder. "Family is more than words, Thomas. We'll figure this out together."

Drake and Miller, observing the meeting, noted the shift in family dynamics. It seemed that the balance of power was beginning to tilt.

After his meeting with Andrew, Thomas went directly to Drake and Miller's room to share something he had overheard regarding Hunt. The detectives watched as he entered with a serious expression.

"Detective, officer," Thomas began, closing the door behind him. "I overheard something a few days ago at home that might help. I accidentally caught part of a conversation Hunt had over the phone."

Edgar nodded, signaling for him to continue. "What exactly did he say?"

Thomas frowned, recalling the details. "Hunt was speaking with someone about a 'mortgage document' that could affect the Lancaster estate. It sounded like he planned to use it as leverage to strengthen his hold over the family."

Miller raised an eyebrow, looking at Edgar. "Another hidden tactic of control, perhaps. It sounds like he left some sort of 'insurance' in case things didn't go as planned."

Edgar exhaled thoughtfully. "We need to locate these documents. If they exist, it could be the proof we need to expose his schemes."

Thomas nodded, understanding the importance of his information. "I thought it might be valuable, so I came to you right away."

"Thank you, Thomas," Edgar replied sincerely. "Every piece like this helps us understand the scope of what's going on here, and the legacy Hunt tried to leave behind."

Feeling his contribution was significant, Thomas nodded and stepped out to give the detectives space to discuss the new insights.

Once Thomas left, Drake and Miller turned to each other to strategize.

"If Hunt really left a mortgage document on the Lancaster estate, it means he was still trying to control them, even after his financial collapse," Edgar noted. "Whatever the case, we have to find that document if it's out there."

Miller nodded pensively. "We've already seen that he set up contingencies, prepared for any outcome. And now, that plan has become a burden weighing down the Lancasters."

They continued their review of the security footage, shifting their focus to the hallway outside Evelyn's room. The screen showed Lucy and Geraldine taking turns visiting her. A few hours into the footage, the doctor was seen examining Evelyn, after which her condition appeared to worsen as he departed.

"We should send a sample of her tea for analysis," Edgar suggested calmly. "It might tell us if something specific triggered her decline."

The lab work took several hours, so Drake and Miller continued their review. On one recording, the camera showed Geraldine carrying a tea tray. As she walked, her phone rang, and she stopped, setting the tray aside to answer.

"Not now—I'm busy. We'll talk later," she said impatiently, pressing the phone to her ear.

Edgar squinted as the recording showed other family members passing by Geraldine in the narrow hallway on their way to dinner. The tray's position allowed anyone to easily approach the teacup unnoticed and tamper with it.

Oliver, Andrew, Amelia, and others were seen passing by.

"So while she was distracted, any one of them could have added something to the tea," Miller observed quietly, eyes fixed on the screen.

Finally, the lab results arrived. Edgar read the report aloud: "Glycoside. The same sedative, but its concentration has doubled." He looked at Miller with concern. "Whoever did this wasn't just taking advantage of an opportunity—they intentionally increased the dose."

Miller nodded, summing it up. "Now we know everyone in the house remains a suspect."

Drake and Miller exchanged glances, thinking about their next steps. Clearly, someone was closely watching the situation and had deliberately added the substance to Evelyn's tea to make her even more vulnerable.

Edgar scanned through the list of suspects displayed on his tablet.

"We need to figure out who in the house has access to this substance," he said thoughtfully. "It's a medical drug, and it's unlikely it ended up here by accident. Could any of them have dealt with such substances before?"

Miller nodded.

"We should ask Evelyn's doctor if he noticed anyone in the family showing an unusual interest in her condition, or if they tried to find out about her prescriptions."

They decided to discuss the lab results with Evelyn's doctor. The following day, when the doctor arrived for her check-up, Drake and Miller waited until he finished his visit and approached him.

"Doctor, thank you for your time," began Edgar. "We'd like to talk to you about the analysis of her tea. We found glycoside in doubled concentration. This substance doesn't usually end up in a drink by accident. Did you notice anything unusual in the family's behavior?"

The doctor looked slightly taken aback by the lab results.

"Glycoside? That's a serious substance, capable of causing extreme weakness and even heart suppression," he said, frowning. "Of course, it's not on my list of prescribed medications. No one from the family directly asked me about her treatment, but Lucy asked several times when her mother might recover. However, that seems natural enough."

"We understand," Miller replied. "It's possible someone else with access to her room may have left something there unnoticed. Doctor, how quickly could glycoside take effect?"

The doctor answered thoughtfully, "Depending on the concentration, it could take effect within a few hours, especially with regular dosing."

After speaking with the doctor, Drake and Miller returned to the camera recordings. Now it was clear to them that someone in the house was deliberately trying to weaken Evelyn, and they had to find out who.

Drake and Miller replayed the footage showing Geraldine carrying the tea tray, slowing down the video to catch any small details. Unfortunately, the family members walking by her briefly blocked the view, preventing them from seeing who might have added the substance.

They decided to try another approach and asked Geraldine to take Evelyn her tea again the next day, instructing her to repeat her previous actions exactly. This time, the detectives carefully set up additional cameras at different angles to cover the hallway fully and eliminate blind spots.

Unaware of their intentions, Geraldine agreed and soon repeated her route to Evelyn's room with the tea tray in hand. Drake and Miller watched the live footage closely, hoping to spot any suspicious movement. Drake called Geraldine at just the moment when others were passing by her on their way to dinner, distracting her with a request to bring dessert afterward. The camera captured nothing unusual.

When they collected the cup for analysis, the results confirmed: only tea was in the cup, with no trace of glycoside; the trap had failed.

"It seems our suspect realized we were watching," Miller remarked, closing the folder with the lab report.

Edgar frowned, realizing the culprit was likely aware of their surveillance and had decided to lay low.

Edgar looked thoughtfully at the monitor showing the camera footage, realizing the suspect might be more cunning than they'd anticipated.

"We'll have to change tactics," he said after a pause, setting the folder aside. "If we're too obvious, they'll find a way to stay hidden. Let's try giving them a distraction, so they feel safe enough to make another mistake."

Miller nodded, considering the idea.

"So, we need to make them relax. We could act as if we've stopped watching. For example, let's announce that we're leaving for a few days to gather information elsewhere, putting the investigation on hold temporarily," he suggested. "That could prompt them to act again."

Edgar nodded approvingly.

"Good idea. We'll stage our departure, while secretly setting up additional hidden cameras to monitor the house remotely. This will allow us to see who acts up when they think we're gone."

That evening, the detectives informed the family members of their temporary departure, claiming they needed to examine documents outside the estate. They explained that it might take time, and they couldn't be sure when they'd return. Observing each person's reaction carefully, they noticed that some family members seemed visibly more relaxed.

After setting up extra equipment, Drake and Miller placed hidden cameras in a few new locations, including previously unmonitored rooms. With remote access, they could now monitor the household from a distance.

The next morning, they drove away, but parked nearby, connected to the surveillance feed, and waited.

Connecting to the surveillance, Drake and Miller patiently monitored the activity in the mansion. On the screen, the residents of the house appeared, each seemingly absorbed in their own matters. Yet, the detectives knew that tension was thick within the family.

At first, the cameras recorded Oliver as he cautiously headed toward the study. Drake and Miller exchanged a look as they noticed him close the door and, after turning on a dim light, begin searching. He quickly glanced over shelves, opened desk drawers, and carefully studied the contents. Finally, he pulled out an old, battered folder, flipping through its pages before pausing on one, then putting the folder back precisely where he had found it.

"Looks like he was after something very specific," Miller commented, leaning closer to the screen.

"It's definitely not just a family archive," Edgar added. "Let's keep watching—this might lead to more clues."

Later, they noticed an exchange in the living room that caught their attention: Lucy and Thomas, who they believed barely knew each other, were engaged in an unusually intense conversation. Lowering her voice, Lucy spoke firmly.

"This has to stay between us. I'm not sure we can trust anyone else. I feel like someone in this house is hiding something, and I intend to find out what."

Thomas paused, then hesitantly nodded. "But if someone suspects we're digging into old matters, it could end badly for us," he warned.

Drake and Miller exchanged glances.

"I wonder how long they've been working together?" Miller asked quietly, keeping his gaze on the screen.

"Clearly, they share a common interest. We need to figure out what they're after," Edgar agreed.

By evening, another scene caught their eye: Oliver, standing in the corridor by Evelyn's room, glanced around, seemingly checking to ensure no one was nearby. Satisfied, he cautiously entered. A few minutes later, he exited, looking around once more, then headed back toward the study.

"This is going too far," muttered Miller. "What possible reason could he have for involving himself in Evelyn's condition?"

Edgar squinted thoughtfully. "It's possible his visit is related to the recent notes we received. Someone in the house is intentionally keeping her weak, and Oliver could be among those involved."

The detectives continued watching, realizing their plans were starting to yield results.

The following morning, as Drake and Miller observed the house via the cameras, they received a message from Martin Hudson, who was in a nearby town. He said he had found crucial documents and requested a meeting at a designated location to share new information in person.

An hour later, they met in a small cafe outside the estate. Martin, tired but focused, handed over several folders containing detailed records on Hunt's and Norrington's dealings, as well as key documents related to the Lancasters.

"These papers were hidden in Hunt's old files," Martin began, pointing to one document marked "Asset Management Trust." "It seems Hunt and Norrington preemptively set up a power of attorney over Lancaster assets in case the main heirs refused to pay on the debts."

Miller frowned, studying the document. "But the Lancasters have no debt to Hunt. How could he force them to pay?"

"That's the cunning part," Martin explained. "Hunt used an old transaction between Richard Lancaster and one of his partners. According to the records, Richard was to provide part of the family's assets in return for a major loan. That loan was settled during Richard's life, but Hunt forged the papers, making it appear that the debt was never repaid."

Edgar listened carefully, processing every word. "So Hunt counted on Richard's passing to leave the Lancasters defenseless, and Norrington could use this false debt to seize the family's property?"

"Exactly," Martin confirmed. "But there's more. These records contain the names of people to whom Hunt sold the fake debt bonds. They're influential business figures, and if one of them decides to pursue the Lancaster assets, they could pose a serious threat."

Edgar glanced at the list of names and paused on "Norrington." He looked at Miller and said, "This explains why Norrington is so keen on these documents. If the debt is confirmed as real, the Lancasters could indeed lose their inheritance."

Martin nodded. "Yes, and it seems Norrington was willing to go to great lengths to ensure these papers never reached the rightful heirs."

Martin laid out the final documents before Drake and Miller, highlighting the fake debt obligations. He stressed that while the Lancasters, in reality, had no outstanding debt, Hunt's fabricated narrative could become a danger to their entire inheritance if certain parties backed it.

"Edgar," Martin began, opening a file, "these are all the falsified obligations Hunt made against the Lancasters. He knew they owed him nothing, but his paperwork makes them look like major debtors. This was his insurance if things ever escalated and he needed a legal basis to ruin the family."

"How does this even work?" Miller asked with a frown. "If the paperwork isn't sufficient proof, how could he coerce them into paying?"

"That's where his plan comes in," Martin explained, pointing to a clause in the agreement. "Hunt arranged a power of attorney for Norrington and other partners who supposedly 'purchased' Lancaster's debt. If recognized, the Lancasters would be forced to pay a vast sum, and Norrington and his allies would become owners of their assets."

Edgar understood the full picture. "So it was critical for Hunt to eliminate any evidence that the debt was fraudulent—and anyone who knew the truth," he concluded. "First was Richard Lancaster, then Peter Grace, their economist…everyone who might expose the forgery or stop it."

Martin nodded, adding, "And we don't know yet who Hunt or his associates might target next. Now we must ask—who else knows the truth about the forgery? And who benefits from keeping this scheme alive after Hunt?"

Edgar noted that the key figures who could still prevent Norrington from exploiting the family and expose his crimes included:

Evelyn Lancaster — As Richard's widow, she might know more than anyone suspects.

Thomas — As a potential heir, he is not only a part of the family but could be a serious obstacle to Norrington if his role as an heir complicates Norrington's plans.

Lucy — Richard's granddaughter. Her intense interest in the family might arouse Norrington's suspicions if she begins to ask questions.

"If their goal is to eliminate every witness," Edgar observed, "then Evelyn and Thomas remain at risk. They are the last who could challenge the forgery and defend the estate."

Miller pondered this, adding, "We also need to uncover how Hunt and Norrington are drawing in allies. They could be manipulating not only the evidence but also individuals in the house. If anyone among the staff or family was promised a reward, they might be complicit in Evelyn's poisoning or in silencing other witnesses."

Edgar nodded. "Our task is to find out who else is tied to Norrington. It could be a family member or someone close to the house. We'll need to heighten surveillance and watch every move."

With this clarity, the detectives knew their time was running short as they followed the trail of Hunt's remaining allies, uncovering new details that would prove crucial.

Drake and Miller realized that the confrontation with Norrington was becoming increasingly complex. The closer they got to the truth, the more dangerous their findings became. They decided to tighten surveillance on all household members, especially on those who might have been involved in Hunt's plans.

By the following morning, the detectives had reconnected to the mansion's surveillance feed after spending the night at a hotel. One by one, the screens showed family members occupied with their daily activities. Their attention was drawn to Amelia's strange movements—she seemed to be carefully avoiding encounters with the other residents. She moved quickly from room to room, pausing occasionally as if deep in thought.

"She seems more nervous than usual," Miller remarked, watching the screen.

"She might be hiding something," Edgar replied quietly, keeping his gaze fixed on the camera.

Later, the detectives observed Amelia leaving the house and heading toward a small shed at the far end of the garden. She took out a key and quickly looked around to ensure she wasn't being followed before unlocking the door and disappearing inside.

"Something's off here," Edgar said, exchanging a knowing look with Miller. "We need to find out what's drawing her to that shed."

A few minutes later, Amelia emerged, locked the door again, and returned to the house. Drake and Miller decided to wait until nightfall to inspect the building. Leaving the cameras running, they carefully made their way to the shed, picked the lock, and slipped inside to discover what Amelia was hiding.

Inside, they found several small boxes of documents and an old cassette recorder with tapes. Edgar switched on one of the tapes, and in the silence, they heard Richard Lancaster's voice:

"If you're listening to this, it means I wasn't able to stop Hunt's plans. He's determined to claim our property by any means. But he has a weakness. There are documents proving he falsified our debts. They're hidden in the house, and only you can find them..."

Drake and Miller exchanged glances, realizing the importance of their discovery. They might have just found the key to unraveling Hunt and Norrington's entire scheme.

"We need to take this and examine it closely," Edgar said, tucking the recorder into his bag. "These documents may hold the evidence the Lancasters need to contest these debts and preserve their inheritance."

They left the shed and returned to the house to continue reviewing the materials and determine who else in the mansion might be involved in this dangerous scheme.

Back inside, Drake and Miller settled into the study to review the documents in a quieter setting. They connected the recorder to a laptop to play the tape and hear every detail more clearly. Richard's voice, though brief and to the point, provided crucial hints:

"If you found this, it means Hunt has put his scheme into action. The falsified debts are hidden among the family records in the library — he inserted them into the financial reports and hid them in the archive. Evelyn and the children know nothing, but if these papers fall into the wrong hands, they could lose everything."

Miller, listening to the recording, frowned.

"This confirms that Richard knew about Hunt's scheme and tried to stop it. But it seems he never got the chance to uncover the forged documents."

Edgar, processing the information, suggested:

"We need to check the library immediately. If those records are still there, they could be definitive evidence against Hunt and Norrington."

They proceeded to the library. Opening the old archive cabinet, Edgar sifted through each document, scanning for unusual entries or forgeries. After a few minutes of careful searching, he pulled out a folder containing debt agreements. Some documents looked strange: they bore Richard's signature, but the papers themselves appeared newer than the rest.

"Found it," Edgar whispered, pulling out the folder. "These show massive debts that Richard allegedly never repaid to Hunt."

Miller glanced at the signatures and immediately pointed out:

"This is a skillful forgery. It looks like Hunt counted on no one examining these papers after Richard's death."

They made copies of the documents and sealed the originals to deliver later to the Lancaster family's attorney.

When the detectives returned to the observation room, they noticed Amelia on one of the cameras again. She was speaking softly on the phone, holding it close to her ear.

"I've got everything ready," she said. "Tonight, we'll finish it. The detectives left, but they could return at any moment."

Drake and Miller exchanged tense glances.

"Looks like someone plans to act tonight," Miller said, watching the screen. "We may catch them in the act."

Edgar nodded.

"It's time for the decisive move. We need to stay here, keep out of sight, and wait for them to show themselves."

Night fell, and Drake and Miller, positioned in different parts of the house, continued monitoring the cameras and their surroundings. The hours ticked by, and tension built up. Finally, close to midnight, a familiar face appeared on the screen—Norrington.

Drake and Miller froze, watching as Norrington slipped into the house. He moved confidently, as if well-acquainted with the layout of the rooms and hallways. Glancing back occasionally to ensure he wasn't being followed, he made his way straight to the library.

"Right to where we found the forged documents," Edgar whispered, observing him on the screen.

Norrington went over to the old archive cabinet. He carefully removed a file, quickly scanned its contents, and, satisfied, replaced it. He then pulled out another document—one of the forged debt agreements—and scrutinized it, as if checking whether it had been tampered with.

Miller signaled to Edgar that it was time to act. Leaving the camera recording, they quietly made their way to the library, taking care not to alert Norrington. Reaching the door, Miller slowly opened it, and they both stepped inside, catching Norrington just as he was reaching into his pocket.

Norrington turned abruptly, meeting their gaze. He tried to maintain a calm expression, though the tension in his eyes betrayed him.

"Didn't expect company this late," he said with a smirk, hiding the documents behind his back.

"And yet, here you are in the house without permission—again," Edgar replied, keeping his eyes fixed on him. "Now, would you care to explain what exactly you were looking for?"

Norrington smirked at him.

"I'm sure proving anything will be challenging. These documents are Lancaster family matters. I'm their official representative, as you know."

Miller, barely concealing his irritation, said coldly:

"An official representative hiding forged debt papers? Doubt that's something the law will overlook."

Norrington clenched his jaw, realizing his plans had unraveled. Instead of backing down, however, he took a tougher stance.

"Do you honestly think you'll be able to prove anything? Hunt was a mastermind in his affairs. Not a single paper, not a single document will leave you with a chance, and soon, this house and the Lancaster estate will be mine."

Unfazed, Edgar replied:

"Unlike you, we already know the truth. And now, it'll become public knowledge."

Norrington paused for a moment, then, holding his gaze, retorted:

"You'll regret this."

Edgar maintained eye contact, watching Norrington closely but keeping any mention of the cameras to himself.

"Your plan has been exposed, Norrington," Edgar said calmly. "Forged debt obligations, fake transactions, attempts to seize Lancaster property. I think you understand that none of this will go unpunished."

Norrington forced a smirk, though tension was evident in his eyes.

"I doubt you'll be able to prove anything. All you have are your assumptions, Edgar. And assumptions hold little weight in my world."

Edgar nodded slowly, as if in agreement, then continued:

"But if my 'assumptions' are so trivial, why are you here? Why resort to forgery and threats against the family? You knew that, with Hunt's death, all control would be in your hands. But here's the catch—we've managed to gather enough to bring down your entire plan."

Meanwhile, Miller, having completed the call, re-entered the room and positioned himself slightly behind Norrington, signaling to Edgar that backup was en route.

"This is the end, Norrington," Edgar said, stepping forward. "Your game is over."

Backup was already entering the house, and officers were heading toward the library.

Drake and Miller exchanged a look, realizing their plan had succeeded. They knew Norrington understood what was happening, though he tried to maintain his composure to the end.

Norrington stood before them, suppressing frustration as he accepted his defeat.

"All you have are pieces of paper," he said icily, looking directly at Edgar. "Your 'guesses' won't amount to anything. And no one will believe you when I claim this house and the Lancaster estate as mine."

Keeping his calm, Edgar replied:

"In another world, maybe, Norrington. But we have more than enough evidence—enough to send you to prison. The documents, the recordings, and your little 'night visit' here have sealed it."

Norrington froze, realizing his position had become untenable. He hesitated briefly, then officers entered the room.

Miller stepped forward and announced:

"Victor Norrington, you're under arrest on suspicion of fraud and forgery of documents in an attempt to seize another's property. You'll have a chance to explain yourself in court."

Grinding his teeth, Norrington silently allowed the officers to place him in handcuffs. A glimmer of confidence remained in his gaze, as though he thought this setback would only be temporary.

Drake and Miller watched as Norrington was escorted out, feeling a sense of satisfaction that their investigation had reached its logical conclusion.

Chapter 13: The Final Exposure

Detective Edgar Drake and Police Officer James Miller organized an important luncheon to gather everyone involved in the recent events surrounding the Lancaster family. They invited the residents of the estate, as well as Hart, Mary, Thomas, and Martin Hudson.

The seating arrangement at the long, meticulously set table was carefully planned by the detectives to convey the seriousness of the discussion ahead. Edgar took his seat next to Amelia, with Miller positioned directly across from him, near the exit, ensuring he could react swiftly if needed. This positioning made it clear that the detectives intended to control the proceedings from both ends of the table.

Hart and Mary sat at one end of the table, somewhat isolated from the family nucleus. Hart's self-assured expression and his deliberately distant seat gave the impression that he saw himself as "above" the situation, though his occasional assessing glances at the others suggested he was carefully watching their reactions.

To Mary's surprise, Thomas chose to sit beside Lucy, hinting at a bond of mutual trust and support between them. Oliver sat beside Thomas, visibly tense, occasionally glancing around as if ensuring everything was under control. Across from him sat Andrew, with Evelyn and Geraldine to his right. Andrew maintained a calm expression, yet his observant gaze missed nothing happening at the table.

The atmosphere resembled the calm before a storm. The guests sat in a mix of anticipation and tension, sensing that a crucial conversation would soon begin, in which secrets would be laid bare and the detectives would unravel the carefully concealed ties and motives.

This was the moment when Drake and Miller could finally shine a light on what linked all these people, putting the final pieces together in the Lancaster case and exposing Hunt and Norrington's schemes.

Edgar cleared his throat, drawing the attention of those gathered. As the murmurs faded, he began, looking around the room.

"Thank you all for coming," he started. "I know tensions have been high in this house over the past weeks, and today is the day to bring clarity to the secrets that have remained hidden. We are close to concluding our investigation, and there are crucial facts you all need to hear."

A quiet tension filled the room as guests exchanged wary glances. Hart, seated slightly apart next to Mary, listened intently. Meanwhile, Miller, sitting by the exit, observed everyone, prepared for any turn of events.

Drake addressed the people sitting at the table:

"Let's start with the main issue. Recent events in this house were no coincidence but part of a well-planned scheme designed to gain control over the Lancaster estate. The mastermind of this scheme is sitting here with us today," Edgar looked pointedly at Hart, and he tensed, meeting the detective's gaze.

"Hart," continued Edgar, "you thought you could go unpunished, but your actions have left too many traces. We know you forged debt obligations to create the appearance that the Lancaster family owed you substantial sums. These documents were hidden among old archives and reports to ensure the family wouldn't suspect anything."

Edgar turned his attention to Oliver, whose expression betrayed his uncertainty.

"Oliver," he addressed, "didn't you realize you were just a pawn in this scheme? Your recent attempts to access the study didn't go unnoticed. We saw you searching through documents, trying to understand what was hidden."

Oliver turned pale, struggling to keep his composure.

"I was just trying to make sure everything was in order," he replied quietly. "I didn't know about Hart's schemes."

Edgar nodded, maintaining eye contact.

"We understand. But now, you know who orchestrated this and why."

Then he turned his attention to Amelia and Mary, who looked tense.

"Amelia," Edgar continued, "your recent trips to the shed also raised questions. Inside, we found records where Richard Lancaster warned of Hart's plans. He tried to protect the family estate but, unfortunately, didn't succeed."

Amelia leaned back in her chair, realizing that her secrets had been uncovered.

Miller added, "And let's not forget Hart's ally—Victor Norrington. With his help, the entire scheme to seize Lancaster property was constructed. We caught Norrington in the act, and we have enough evidence for his arrest."

At this, Hart, who had been silent until now, raised his head.

"Wait," he tried to protest. "These accusations are just words. You have no proof against me."

Edgar nodded calmly.

"But we do have proof," he said. "We have records, documents, and witness statements that corroborate everything we're saying."

The guests exchanged glances, fully grasping the weight of the charges.

After a pause to let everyone absorb what they'd heard, Edgar resumed with conviction:

"All of these schemes and forged documents were part of a plot to gain control over the Lancaster estate. It wasn't just about fake debt obligations. Behind these actions lay manipulation, betrayal, threats, and even attempts to harm others."

Mary, seated next to Hart, looked at him in confusion, then at Thomas, who sat with Lucy. It was clear she was only now beginning to understand what had been happening around her and her family.

Continuing where Drake left off, Miller added:

"As for the methods Hart used to undermine the Lancasters, we discovered records of a substance that was used to poison Evelyn. According to lab tests, it was this substance that caused her severe illness. Someone sought to weaken her physically and mentally so she couldn't resist. And let's not forget, essential documents challenging the debt were bequeathed to her."

Evelyn, seated at the end of the table, lowered her head, coming to terms with everything she had endured.

At this moment, Hart, seeing that his plan was fully exposed, tried one last defense:

"And yet, your claims are unsupported. Yes, I worked with Richard, and yes, there were unresolved obligations. But this is business. Without concrete evidence, all these statements are just slander."

Drake looked at Miller and calmly responded,

"You're wrong, Hart. We have more than enough proof. Your manipulations are documented, and with Norrington's testimony, which we've secured, everything is now clear. We also have video and audio recordings detailing your plans and schemes, including your attempts to bribe family members to make everything appear legitimate."

Lucy, who had been silent until now, looked directly at Hart and said,

"You tried to make us all distrust each other, to divide us. But in the end, the truth came out."

Thomas, sitting beside her, nodded in agreement.

"It's not just talk, Hart. Now I know I made the right choice in supporting Lucy and Andrew. We're protecting our heritage."

Edgar concluded,

"Today, this long-awaited resolution has arrived. You, Hart, will face charges of fraud, forgery, and conspiracy. We'll make sure that everything you've done doesn't go unpunished."

A tense silence fell over the room as everyone watched Hart struggle to contain his anger, realizing that his carefully crafted plan was falling apart in front of everyone. Officers, called ahead of time, entered the room and stood behind Hart, ready to make the arrest.

Edgar, looking directly at Hart, continued,

"All your fake debt obligations, all your forged documents—they're now evidence against you. Your attempts to dominate the Lancasters will no longer remain hidden. This is the end, Hart."

Hart lost his composure and shouted in frustration,

"What do you know about the truth? All you have are guesses! You won't prove anything, do you hear? All of this—belongs to me! By right, it's mine!"

Miller took a step forward,

"We have more than enough evidence to expose you in court. And your 'right' will soon be used as proof against you."

The officers placed handcuffs on Hart. He struggled briefly but knew that resistance was futile. His gaze darted around the room, searching for support, but none of the guests responded.

As they began to lead Hart away, Edgar added, holding his gaze,

"You ordered more than one death in this house."

Hart turned back, smirking, shaking his head, and with a sly smile said,

"Oh, but the one who executed the orders is still here with you in this room."

Hart's smug grin remained as he was led out, his final words hanging in the air, leaving everyone in the room exchanging wary looks.

Andrew lifted his glass, taking a sip, and Mary followed suit, glancing around at the guests. Drake turned to address everyone, saying,

"I'm giving the accomplice and executor a chance to confess voluntarily. This will be taken into account by the court. So, while you still have a moment…"

He paused, then pulled an old childhood photo of Thomas from a folder and handed it to Evelyn. On the back was Richard's message: "Please accept him into the family. I didn't do it in time due to my own cowardice."

Evelyn studied the photo for a long moment before looking up at Thomas. She handed the picture to Mary and quietly said,

"We've already accepted him into the family."

Drake nodded in approval and continued:

"Evelyn, let's start with you. You were deliberately poisoned. Had you taken more of that substance, you wouldn't be with us today. And those shoes—dirty and clearly not your size—that were neatly placed by your bed to make it seem as though you'd been out in the garden at night? They were planted there."

Evelyn listened, processing the revelation, while the others sat in stunned silence. Edgar took a breath and added,

"They targeted you because you knew too much. Your romantic involvement with Norrington left no room for doubt. You knew Richard's death wasn't accidental. He passed away shortly after a conversation with Norrington."

Gasps spread through the room as everyone turned to Evelyn in shock.

Evelyn slowly raised her gaze, gathering her thoughts before she spoke.

"I knew that Norrington insisted on certain 'business' with Richard, but I never thought it would go this far… By the time I realized he was using me, it was too late. Richard had suspected him, but he didn't want to endanger the family."

Andrew, seated next to her, frowned.

"So you knew his intentions and didn't warn us?" he asked, his voice a mix of frustration and confusion.

Evelyn nodded, looking at him with regret.

"I thought I could fix it on my own. But Norrington was far too clever. He knew exactly how to keep me under his control and threatened that if I spoke up, the consequences would affect all of you."

Edgar listened carefully, then added when she fell silent:

"Richard left notes warning that your ties with Norrington could spell disaster for the entire family. He knew Norrington was a threat and would stop at nothing to get everything he wanted."

Evelyn lowered her head, then gathered her resolve and spoke again.

"I understand now that his plans were always far more extensive than I realized. I was just a pawn."

Drake addressed those gathered in the room:

"Someone in this house helped him, whether knowingly or suspecting his motives. Now, we have a choice: give this person a chance to confess voluntarily or bring everything to light in court, where all the facts will be exposed."

At this moment, Geraldine, who had been sitting quietly and observing, suddenly flinched and paled slightly. Edgar noticed her discomfort.

"Geraldine, is there something you'd like to say?" he asked, his voice gentle but firm.

She licked her lips and lowered her gaze, barely whispering:

"I... I helped Norrington several times. He assured me it was necessary for the family's safety. He convinced me he was doing it for all of us."

Her confession sent a wave of shock through the room.

Edgar gave her a moment, letting her gather herself and continue.

"I..." her voice shook, and she looked down for a moment. "A few times, I helped Norrington get into the house at night by leaving the library window latch unlocked. He said he was searching for documents that would save the Lancasters and that these papers would supposedly help protect the family's inheritance. I believed him..."

Evelyn looked at Geraldine in disbelief.

"You thought you were helping us?" she whispered, still stunned.

"Yes," Geraldine nodded. "But when he asked me to put muddy shoes under your bed," she glanced at Evelyn, "I refused. That's when I realized Norrington had ulterior motives, something that wasn't in our best interests. I stopped speaking to him and made sure all the windows were locked so he couldn't get in again."

Miller, watching Geraldine's confession, leaned back, exchanging a brief look with Edgar.

Edgar then addressed the room.

"It seems that Norrington manipulated not only the financial documents but also people to gain their trust. And those who trusted him"—his gaze lingered on Geraldine—"thought they were serving the family's interests, only to become pawns in his ruthless scheme."

A heavy silence filled the room as each person felt the weight of these newly uncovered secrets.

Edgar looked around, letting everyone absorb what they'd heard.

"Would anyone else like to add anything?" he asked, offering a final chance for any remaining truths to come forward.

Thomas leaned forward slightly and, glancing at Lucy, exhaled quietly.

"I think it's time I shared what I found out," he began. "A few days ago, I overheard Norrington discussing some 'insurance' in case his plan failed. He mentioned certain papers that would supposedly guarantee him control over our property if the Lancaster family couldn't contest the debt obligations."

Mary, who had remained silent until now, gasped.

"You knew about this? Why didn't you tell us?"

Thomas met her gaze calmly.

"Because until the last moment, I didn't know whom I could trust in this house. Now I understand that it wasn't just about Norrington or Hant—everyone here has somehow been caught up in their web."

Drake nodded, acknowledging Thomas's honesty.

"Thank you, Thomas. What you've shared corroborates what we've already learned."

Then, addressing the entire family, Edgar continued:

"Norrington's 'insurance policies' were forged for one purpose—to completely ruin the Lancasters and take over their inheritance. However, we now have enough evidence to ensure that you will reclaim everything that rightfully belongs to you."

Edgar held a pause, intensifying the atmosphere, then continued, casting a piercing glance around the table.

"Let's return to Evelyn," he said. "All of this information about Evelyn's connection with Norrington was also known to Simon. He was aware of Hunt's schemes as well and tried to resist him without involving you all. But it cost him dearly."

Drake's words stunned everyone into silence. Geraldine turned pale, gripping the edge of the table.

"Geraldine, you knew Simon; you saw how tense he was," Edgar continued. "But due to your strained relationship, he couldn't fully trust you. Simon knew too much. He knew about Hunt's and Norrington's plans for the Lancaster fortune and even about Thomas. But this dangerous information became too heavy a burden."

Drake paused again, and everyone waited tensely for his next words.

"Richard did not die a natural death," he said firmly. "On Simon's laptop, there's a report from a doctor he hired, concluding that Richard's death was deliberate. Richard was murdered. That's why he became the first victim in the chain of events that led us here. And Simon was the second."

Mary gasped, covering her mouth, unable to process what she was hearing.

"The third victim was Peter Grace, your family's financial adviser," Edgar continued, looking each person in the eye. "And the fourth was supposed to be Evelyn. But we intervened and disrupted their plans, saving her life."

Evelyn sat frozen, staring ahead, still trying to comprehend the revelation.

"And Martin Hudson was also in danger," Edgar went on. "Your family's lawyer, who sincerely sought to protect the Lancaster legacy. We sent him on a fact-finding mission to keep him safe. Thanks to his efforts, we found the genuine documents that confirmed Hunt's fraudulent schemes."

Martin nodded silently, and Edgar cast a sharp look around the room once more.

"So, we can cross Evelyn and Martin off the list," he concluded.

Drake once again scanned the tense faces at the table before he continued:

"So, we've identified those who were targeted and those who have already fallen victim to their plan. But someone in this house may still be connected to Norrington's schemes. And despite Hunt's exposure, the remaining participants could still carry on his work."

Everyone in the room froze, hanging on the detective's words. Andrew placed his glass down and leaned forward.

"You mean the danger isn't over yet?"

Edgar nodded calmly.

"Exactly. As we've seen, this plan didn't depend on one person alone. Those who could reveal the truth about Hunt and Norrington's machinations were being eliminated one by one. Fortunately, they didn't manage to finish the job."

Miller added, "We've concluded that someone else in this house knew more than the rest and was covering for Norrington — possibly while hiding the true motives for their actions."

Lucy, who had been silent until now, suddenly broke the silence:

"If anyone here is still connected to these schemes, isn't now the time to tell it all? The more we keep hidden, the more danger we're all in."

Drake nodded in agreement, signaling that he supported her point.

"Exactly why we're giving a chance for voluntary confession. Anyone who has something to share that could help in this investigation or shed light on Norrington's plans, now is the time to speak up."

The room was plunged into a heavy silence.

"Well, then, has Hunt's accomplice decided to confess yet?" Edgar Drake asked, scanning the room with a sharp gaze. The tension in the room had reached its peak.

Geraldine couldn't hold back and blurted out, "It wasn't me!" which elicited a few quiet chuckles, slightly easing the atmosphere.

"Stop dragging it out," Evelyn said, looking directly at Edgar. "I want to know who killed my husband."

Edgar nodded and began explaining, "At the start of our investigation, we chased someone who jumped out of the window. Later, we found footprints — women's footprints. They matched the shoes that, as we discovered, were found under your bed, Evelyn. I suggest the ladies try them on to determine exactly who they belong to."

Amelia sighed, gathering her courage, and admitted, "They're my shoes," she said firmly, "but I didn't put them under Evelyn's bed."

Drake nodded. "Correct. Norrington planted them there when he secretly visited Evelyn while she was on bed rest. But Amelia, why did you have to jump out the window yourself?"

Amelia hesitated but replied, "I was conducting my own investigation and got scared that I'd be killed, that's all."

Detective looked at her intently, catching her unease as she struggled to mask her tension.

"You claim you were simply investigating and feared for your life," he said, tilting his head slightly as if expecting her response. "But let me ask, why did you need to investigate anything at all? There are professionals in the house — we're here to uncover the truth. And you, Amelia, aren't family. What personal gain could you have had?"

Amelia held her breath, her gaze darting nervously around the room, but she said nothing. Drake, sensing they were nearing the climax, turned slightly toward Miller, who handed him a thin folder, as if prepared for this exact moment.

"Moreover," Edgar continued softly but with a steely firmness, "we obtained your phone records. The operators kindly provided us with all the information at my colleague's request. And do you know what they revealed?"

He paused, and the guests at the table, holding their breath, watched him intently.

"They showed that you called… Hunt. Repeatedly."

With those words, Edgar lifted his gaze to her, and a wave of tension swept through the room.

Mary jumped up, her face pale, her lips trembling with restrained anger.

"So it was you… you snake!" she spat with disdain, clenching her fists. "You were connected with him all along?"

Amelia remained silent, pale and seemingly unfocused, while everyone in the room looked at her, understanding that her involvement in the conspiracy was now exposed.

Drake fixed his gaze on her, his expression merciless, his voice cold and sharp as a blade.

"Amelia," he said, holding her gaze, "you weren't merely an accomplice; you were Hunt's enforcer. He promised you wealth, support, loyalty, and it appears you accepted," his words hung in the air like a death sentence. "Your actions speak for themselves. You are the reason Richard is dead. And Simon too."

Amelia paled, as if witnessing her own sentencing, yet she tried to maintain her composure. Her gaze darted around, searching for an escape.

"You even helped to send Peter Grace to his death," Edgar continued without breaking eye contact. "Staging your own 'injury,' you made sure to be in the hospital that day to complete the deed. How did that happen? Ah, yes, initially, Norrington attacked Peter when he realized Peter had uncovered the plans he and Hunt had devised and was about to expose them."

Amelia barely whispered, "That… that's a lie…"

But her voice trembled, and fear shone in her eyes, betraying the truth.

Drake tilted his head thoughtfully and continued, pausing heavily.

"And that's not all. You poisoned Evelyn when you had the chance. You waited until Geraldine brought her tea, then secretly slipped poison into the cup," his words were clear and ruthless, striking with precision. "Did you think no one would notice? Unfortunately for you, Ms. Amelia, our specialists carefully reviewed the camera footage. They found what an ordinary eye might miss, what could easily escape notice. On the recording, it's visible how your hand discreetly adds a powder to Evelyn's cup."

Amelia froze, as if turned to stone, her face distorted with horror. Her gaze was filled with despair — she had nowhere to run, nothing to hope for. She realized that her every move was uncovered, and the game was over.

Geraldine cautiously broke the silence, slightly easing the tension.

"Wait," she began, raising her eyebrows. "Then who threatened me with a knife? I screamed when I saw a shadow with a knife that then jumped out the window… Was that Amelia?"

Drake shook his head, looking at Geraldine.

"No, that was Norrington. Your connection with him ended the moment you refused his request. So, to intimidate you and force you to stay silent, he took matters into his own hands and resorted to threats."

Geraldine shuddered, recalling the terrifying moment, and quietly said, "I had no idea it was all so dangerous."

Drake nodded and, after a pause, looked around at everyone seated at the table.

"The picture is clear now. This house held too many secrets, endangering the Lancaster family and those trying to protect it."

Miller stood up from the table, glancing at everyone, then looked directly at Amelia, who was struggling to remain composed, though her pale face betrayed fear and confusion.

"Amelia Hart," he said firmly, "you are under arrest on suspicion of involvement in schemes to seize the Lancaster family's assets, as well as in aiding and abetting a criminal conspiracy."

Amelia flinched as the officers entered the room. They approached her soundlessly from behind, and before she could say anything, cold handcuffs clicked onto her wrists. She tried to maintain her dignity, but her face showed anxiety and confusion.

As the officers approached her, she tried to keep her composure, but her hands trembled slightly, and a shadow of fear flashed in her eyes. Drake stepped forward, his gaze stern and unyielding.

"Amelia Hart," he pronounced, pausing for emphasis, "you knew that anyone who stood in your way would become a victim. You didn't just help Norrington and Hunt; you killed. You were an executor, a puppet in the hands of those hungry for power."

For a moment, Amelia raised her chin, attempting to preserve her grandeur, but her trembling lips betrayed her. She looked away, but Evelyn, standing nearby, didn't let her avoid it.

"Your family is worthless without money," Amelia hissed, looking at Evelyn with disdain. "And you don't deserve it."

Evelyn replied calmly, almost coldly, "You are envious and cruel, Amelia. And you will answer for everything."

Andrew, unable to hold back his anger, shouted, "How could you, Amelia? My father trusted you…" His voice rang with pain, anger, and disappointment.

Amelia merely shrugged, looking at him with slight contempt.

"The trust of the wealthy," she smirked, "is worth nothing. You're all nothing without your capital."

Those words, dripping with venom, hung in the air. Oliver, who had remained silent until then, could no longer contain himself. He lifted his head and spoke coldly, "Shut up, you snake. Look at what we nurtured on our chest, and you bit us with your poison."

Amelia glared at him with disdain but said nothing. She realized that everyone around her — the Lancasters, the officers — had turned away from her forever.

Mary, who had remained silent, stepped forward, unable to hide her anger.

"So all this betrayal was for greed?" she exclaimed. "You destroyed two families, sent men to jail and to the grave, all for money?"

Amelia looked at her with a disdainful smirk but said nothing. She simply turned away, showing her indifference, as if the accusations and consequences didn't concern her. That cold, indifferent silence had more impact than any words.

Drake gave a subtle nod to the officers, and they led Amelia out. The echo of her heels faded into silence as she slowly left the room, like a ghost of what remained in the past.

With her final step over the threshold, a hush settled, marking the end of a long and painful chapter. A new day was dawning, and with it, a new life awaited those who remained.

Printed in Great Britain
by Amazon

57290452R00152